"The first time I saw Justin p[erform]... graphic, nasty, insolent, and [...] watching. I couldn't stop liste[ning...]
—**Philip Kan Gotanda,**
    playwright and author of No More Cherry Blossoms

"Justin Chin joyously picks at the scab of these times to peek at what our flesh really looks like underneath...no subject is off-limits as Chin humorously explores the hot buttons of sex, class, race, and even proctology!"
—**Tim Miller,**
    performance artist and author of Body Blows

"Justin Chin is a terrifying original. His wit is fierce and biting. He scrutinizes the world in which we live with unrelenting harshness and at the same time with an astounding beauty. A potent and singular voice, Justin Chin has an assured place in American and Asian literature, poetry, and performance."
—**Chay Yew,**
    playwright and director

Attack
of the Man-Eating Lotus Blossoms

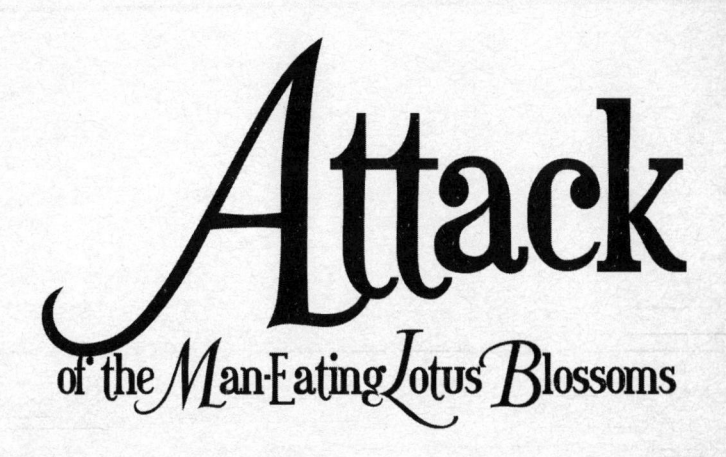

Attack
of the Man-Eating Lotus Blossoms

Justin Chin

suspect thoughts press
www.suspectthoughtspress.com

This book is a work of fiction. Names, characters, places, and incidents are either products of the author's imagination or are used fictitiously. Any resemblance to actual events, locales, or persons, either living or dead, is entirely coincidental.

Copyright © 2005 by Justin Chin

All rights reserved. Except for brief passages quoted in newspaper, magazine, radio, television, or online reviews, no part of this book may be reproduced in any form or any means, electronic or mechanical, including photocopying, recording, or information or retrieval system, without the permission in writing from the publisher.

Cover image and design by Shane Luitjens/Torquere Creative
Book design by Greg Wharton/Suspect Thoughts Press
Special "recipe" design on pg. 91 thanks to Kathleen Pratt
First Edition: August 2005
10 9 8 7 6 5 4 3 2 1

Library of Congress Cataloging-in-Publication Data

Chin, Justin, 1969-
  Attack of the man-eating lotus blossoms / by Justin Chin.
    p. cm.
  ISBN 0-9746388-8-9 (pbk.)
  1. Asian Americans--Drama. 2. Popular culture--United States--Drama. I. Title.

PS3553.H48973A95 2005
812'.54--dc22

2005003755

Suspect Thoughts Press
2215-R Market Street, #544, San Francisco, CA 94114-1612
www.suspectthoughtspress.com

Suspect Thoughts Press is a terrible infant hell-bent to burn the envelope by publishing dangerous books by contemporary authors and poets exploring provocative social, political, queer, spiritual, and sexual themes.

Acknowledgments

In the ten years that I was doing performance work, I had the pleasure of working at many amazing art spaces, some of which are no longer around, and many of which are struggling to stay afloat. I would like to thank all the performance spaces, galleries, curators, administrators, and organizers who invited me and so graciously allowed me to act out all my madnesses in the guise of art. Thanks to: Josie's Cabaret & Juice Joint, the Asian Art Museum, the LAB, the Bearded Lady Truck Stop and Coffee House, Luna Sea Women's Performance Project, Yerba Buena Center for the Arts, 848 Community Artspace, Artists' Television Access, Southern Exposure Gallery, Asian American Theatre Company, New Conservatory Theatre Center, Small Press Distribution, Jon Sims Center for the Performing Arts, Potrero Nuevo Art Fund/New Langton Art, The Walter McBean Gallery at the San Francisco Art Institute, Epicenter Zone, Intersection for the Arts, and KBBK studios (in San Francisco); Highways Performance Space, East West Players, the Mark Taper Forum's Asian Theatre Workshop, and the Japanese American Cultural and Community Center (in Los Angeles); the Cleveland Performance Art Festival; the Sydney Gay & Lesbian Mardi Gras; Franklin Furnace and P.S. 122, Dixon Place, and the Asian American Writers Workshop (in New York); the MacKinney Avenue Contemporary (in Dallas); Works Gallery (in San Jose); Celebration Theatre (in Palm Springs); the Gay Lesbian Bisexual Student groups, the Asian-American Student groups and their faculty advisors at Loyola University, Hampshire College, Stanford University, University of California at Riverside; the University of Hawaii at Manoa English Department and the board of the Joseph Keene Chadwick Memorial Lecture.

For financial support (and morale boost when I needed it), I am especially grateful to the Franklin Furnace Grant for Performance Art, and the Asian American Arts Foundation Grant.

To all the folks who came to my shows, willingly or dragged

screaming and kicking against your will, I thank you.

Finally, this whole trip would have been so bleedingly dull, or surely spun off into insanity, if not for collaborators, friends, and fellow performers who have inspired, assisted, and provided a place to sleep or bitch or celebrate. I thank: Hung Nguyen, Chay Yew, Stacey Makishi, Luis Alfaro, Denise Uyehara, Brighde Mullins, Elliot Linwood, Ming Ma, Lisa Asagi, R. Zamora Linmark, Lüch Linmark, Richard Labonté, Lori Takayesu, Morgan Blair, Alan Reade, Charlie Bergengren, Barnes, Robert Glick, Tim Miller, Holly Hughes, Nao Bustamante, Keith Hennessey, Peggy Shaw and Lois Weaver/ Split Britches, the Medea Project, and everyone whom I've shared a bill, a stage, a platform, a foothold, a stronghold, or a stranglehold with.

I must also thank Dave Thomson, without whom I would not have been able to do a lot of this work.

Inevitably, I'll have neglected to thank someone or another in these acknowledgments. If I've left you out, I apologize. My shaky memory is ever so shaky, and the omission was unintentional (except for the two people who have so royally and irredeemably pissed me off.)

Some of the writing in this collection was previously published, in slightly different forms, in: *The Outlaw Bible of American Poetry*, Alan Kaufman, ed. (Thunder's Mouth Press: 1999); *Rice: Explorations into Asian Gay Culture & Politics*, Song Cho, ed. (Queer Press Community Publishing: 1998); *XCP: Cross Cultural Poetics*; and *Traffic Report*.

For Henry

&

In memoriam,
Donald Montwill

Contents

Hello,...   13

Go, or, The Approximate Infinite Universe
of Mrs. Robert Lomax   19

And Judas Boogied Until His Slippers Wept   47
    Who the Fuck Am I?   49
    Fagtown   50
    97-CHINK, or, Baby, How Do I Look Tonight?   55
    Damage   71
    Calculating the Velocity of Fabulousness 77

Attack of the Man-Eating Lotus Blossoms   83
    A(nthro)pology   85
    Mis-Translations   88
    Happier Talk   91
    Pandora's Box of Shrimp Chow-Fun   91
    Happy Fun Karaoke Time   100
    An Exotic Folk Tale from Far Away   100
    Missionary Positions   103

Holy Spook   109

These Nervous Days   127

Born   145

Advice for Tragic Queens at Home & Abroad   169
    Monkey   169
    Stop All That Insanity   170

Mea Culpa	173
Go-Go GO!	176
I, Documentary	179
The Sarong Party Gay Boy	182
So Solo	189
Butterfly	189

Little Demons
(Odd Bits and Unrealized Performance Pieces)   193
    Slab   193
    From Cockfight   194
    Demon Share (a speculative performance)   198

Hello,...

This is twenty-five years from now: I am sitting in the living room with family and friends. A meal is being prepared and brought to the table, there are clusters of conversation, nephews and nieces are scampering around, a television documentary about the 1990s has just ended.

"Uncle Justin," a niece pipes up. "What was it like in the '90s? What did you do in the '90s?"

"Did you do that funny dance with the glowing sticks at the rave?" a nephew asks. Another nephew joins in, "Did you lose billions in the dot-com bust?"

By now, everyone is focused on this conversation. Lisa gathers all the young ones and seats them in front of me. She chuckles. "In the last decade of the last century, your uncle was a performance artist."

The kids look blankly at me; two of the older ones look horrified. "Oh yes, remember the time you sang off-key renditions of "MacArthur Park" accompanied by tablas?" my brother says. "Or the time you sat in the storefront window with a hood on taking pictures of passersby and people who looked in?"

Zack is laughing as he remembers, "The time you explained gay sex using sock puppets, a dropper, and packets of McDonald's half-and-half." By this time, homosexuality is such the norm that it is passé, we don't have to skirt the topic around little children anymore.

I raise a limp defense. "I was investigating Daddy-boy relationships and how the community..."

"Then there was all those scratched slides and tapes of disembodied sound," Richard says. "Didn't one reviewer say it was the bleakest theatrical experience in recent memory?"

"That was about the...," I try to counter, but I am interrupted by my mom.

"And then there was that bloodletting," she says.

"You're being reductive! There was more to it than just that," I protest.

"And you burned all those T-shirts and made someone write his name on your ass," a voice chimes in from somewhere behind.

"Who's that? Who's over there?" I ask, but no one pays any attention to me.

"You tape-recorded me saying I wanted to oof Magnum PI's hairy chest," Lüch accuses. "And you had all those slides of people's poo-holes, it was gross."

"So, Uncle Justin," another niece sweetly asks, "What's the difference between performance art and making a fool of yourself in public?"

"That's an easy one," I tell the little ones as they follow me when I walk over to bookshelf. "See for yourselves..."

***

From 1992 to the early bits of 2001, I had a concurrent life as a performance artist. I stumbled into performance art quite by accident. I knew what it was and I knew I enjoyed it as a spectator and a consumer, but I never thought I'd would actually do it.

The early '90s was a different time. (Which isn't saying anything at all since every time is a different time.) In the United States, twelve years of a conservative government had taken its toll, a proposal to restrict funds to art that was deemed obscene was in the air, propelled by the rescinding of funds to four artists, the economy was plodding along shakily, and though we did not know it then, because of all the funerals and grief and caring for loved ones, the bell sounding round one of the AIDS epidemic was approaching.

In San Francisco, ACT UP had imploded and Queer Nation too, as they would all over the country. The words "queer studies" and "postmodern" were bandied about and there was a big interest in critical theory and cultural studies. For the first time in recent memory, a presidential candidate had mentioned the words "gays and lesbians" on the campaign trail and *not* in a despicable manner.

You can see how, in this climate, solo performance as an art form, especially within the queer community, made an impact. How using the body, as medium and as content and as form, made such simple and powerful sense. How memory

Attack of the Man-Eating Lotus Blossoms

and remembering was a political act.

Circumstances leading to others, I was somehow given the opportunity to put on a show. As a fledgling writer at that time, I had for a period of two years decided that I would *not* turn down any artistic offer — readings, offers to publish, calls for submissions, offers to perform, anything — that was put to me. And I followed through. And yes, there are a few things that I'm glad are long forgotten by now.

I suspected all along that I was a bad actor, and coming to the United States, this was proved to me. Not only was I a bad actor, I was a bad ethnic actor, threatening to bring down the race with my ineptness.

I discovered that Performance was not like Acting at all, even though there were some elements of Acting in Performance, and there were threads to the Theater. Performance was, in a way, un-Acting, and consciously so too. Whereas Acting, when executed in its highest order, tends toward unconsiously un-Acting. The confusions I think I had about performance art came from whether I followed its history from the European '20s, the Dadaist, Futurist and Surrealist schools, or from the American '60s, of happenings, actions, environmental and Pop art schools. Added to the confusion was the media representation of the stereotypical performance artist, either wailing like a banshee and throwing food at the audience or being pretentious and meaning-challenged, scoffing at idiots who did not get The Meaning when there was none.

My performance work happily embraced everything it could get its grubby hands on. Often described as interdisciplinary, it was more antidisciplinary. Though presented in theater settings and often under the aegis of theater, it had less to do with the theater, its history and traditions, and was more aligned to that of conceptual art and performance studies.

My performance aesthetics tended to be lo-fi; this was as much a preference as it was a necessity, working with no budget and being mostly self-funded, as many artists are. I learned how to do things cheaply without sacrificing too much of the look or the function. I learned how to make media, slides, video, sounds with what equipment I had, broken or partly-working as it was, or what I could borrow. My iMac was still years away, and I think of all the possibilities that could have been. I saved money and frequent flyer miles for a travel fund. I worked jobs and a schedule that allowed me to do my art. Again, all this is nothing many artist haven't done, aren't doing right now.

Through it all, I was often prodded to do work that was more commercially viable in its form and content. Not that I was deliberately going against that. I knew what sort of narratives and forms were viable, and that I could do it. But that work just didn't hold all that much interest for me. *This* was how I thought, what went on in my head, how I wanted to do it, what I could do based on ability, resources, budget. *This* was how it would be a challenge to me, and how I could have pleasure and enjoyment from doing it.

Some of these performances were successful, some were miseries. I've always felt that I could have staged them better, performed them just a little better.

I am still not a good, or even remotely capable, actor; every time I see good theater, I'm reminded of that. I probably wasn't even a good performer. If anything I trusted that my texts and the overarching ideas of the performance would see me through.

But time passes, and deciding to stay in San Francisco (a decision I made not for love of The City but for other reasons; a decision I do not regret, by the way) made it increasingly difficult to have a life as a performance artist. It was harder to get a run of shows, and I was getting more reluctant to do one-off shows, not to mention the fatigue and exhaustion that puts on a body. After what was to be my last performance, one that was so perfect in my mind, one I truly enjoyed performing, I knew at that moment, sitting on the lanai with my best friends overlooking the Pacific Ocean, that it was the end of that part of my life; and I was happy to end it.

The texts collected here represent the major bulk of the work in my short performance-art life.

In compiling and editing them for this book, I set out some guidelines for myself. First, I would not try to rewrite the

Attack of the Man-Eating Lotus Blossoms

pieces, even as much as I wanted to. As most writers know, you can keep Leavesing of Grassing until you turn to fungus. What I had in hand were working scripts: they had blank spots for ad-libs and improvisations to factor in certain topical cultural and political references, technical information, notes to myself of things to bear in mind during performance. That text was meant to be spoken, verbalized, acted upon, and so I tried to mediate all that into something that can be read, that works as a reading thing, but also as a text that performs.

Secondly, I wanted to provide some anecdotes about the performance of the work, but I did not want to find myself explaining what the work was about. Nothing, and I mean *nothing*, makes you look so much the plonker as when you do that (except actually plonking, of course).

The first point proved to be more difficult than I could imagine. How you write and think now is different from how you wrote and thought ten years ago. The pricks that you were kicking against have either:

1. gone away,
2. been replaced by their understudies, peers, underlings, disciples, demon-spawn,
3. retired or are no longer pricking,
4. become your friend, acquaintance, buddy, or,
5. your shin splints have forced you to stop kicking, or,
6. you've ceded your spot to someone else who is now doing the kicking instead, or
7. you decided to stop kicking and to ask nicely and the pricks were less so, and they listened, and you listened, and a nice chat was had over tea and cakes, and everyone got on and along.

※※※

So, I tell the little ones, "There is this book, that will explain everything to you and more." I pluck the book off the shelf. They gather around as I settle into the comfy chair. I turn to the first page. "Okay, are you ready...?"

GO
OR, THE APPROXIMATE INFINITE UNIVERSE OF MRS. ROBERT LOMAX
"THE RAW STUFF OF SERIOUS RISK-TAKING ... CHIN'S GOING TO BE A MAJOR THEATRE VOICE ..."
— SF BAY TIMES
QUEER WRITER / PERFORMER
JUSTIN CHIN
IN HIS NEW SOLO PERFORMANCE
"JUSTIN CHIN'S STORIES ON BEING A GAY ASIAN-AMERICAN ARE FUNNY, TOUCHING, A BIT SEEDY, SOMETIMES RIBALD."
—SAN JOSE MERCURY NEWS
MAY 11-22 WED-SUN 8PM $10-12
JOSIE'S CABARET & JUICE JOINT 3583 16TH STREET SF RESERVATIONS: 861.7933

Go, or, The Approximate Infinite Universe of Mrs. Robert Lomax (1994-1995)

Let's set the record straight. I was never offended by the movie *The World of Suzie Wong*. I was extremely irritated by it, and on a few occasions, bemused, but never quite so much as offended. Maybe in order to be offended, I would have had to, in some infinitesimal way, believe that the movie's prevalent mythology was viable in my life. It's not. Also, viewing the movie as camp takes some of the sting out, for me at least.

But it must be viable in someone's life: Suzie Wong has become an adjective as well as a verb.

There are bars or lounges named Suzie Wong in Portland, Bangkok (of course), Hanoi (why not?), Beijing (okay...), Mumbai (huh?), Puerto Vallarta (wha...?), and at least eight in Germany, and possibly loads more waiting around the corner.

There is a cocktail (and all of you tittering at that very sophomoric pun, for shame!) called a Suzie Wong: vodka, mandarin liqueur, lemon juice, and champagne.

And there is a variety of lily named Suzie Wong. Guess what color it is?

In promoting the show, slated to begin its run at Josie's Cabaret and Juice Joint in San Francisco, I was lectured by all those in-the-know and in-charge that in order to perk the potential audience's interest, I needed "sexy photos" on the flyer. "Show some flesh," they said. Okay, I thought, there's not much to work with here, but let's see what we can choke up; which in my case, ended up looking like mutton dressed as mutton dressed as something that may not have been lamb.

I never should have listened to that tired age-old gay tenet, which has been used to sell everything from cheese to condoms to Hepatitis booster shots to luxury cars to social equality.

The only thing sex sells is itself.

But as it turned out, I needn't have bothered.

The show I originally conceived was somewhat minimal, a

lot of keeping still and holding positions. For the Chorus, I had initially conceived of having a series of eight or nine actions, performed gestures, that I would repeat over the recorded text; and each time the Chorus reappeared and spoke, the actions were meant to take on a meditative, grounding effect, a familiar touchstone as the content of the Chorus' speech grew more grievous.

On opening night, an awful realization hit: things that I had rehearsed and thought were working just weren't. More than that, everything went to shit. And I only had myself to blame.

Overnight I insanely worked and retooled the entire show and the next night it was completely different, a rougher version of what is represented here. But the damage had been done. The manager relied on his alcoholic co-dependent best friend to tell me that they were yanking more than half my run, and replacing it with local stand-up comics, hyuk-hyuks rushed in saved the day.

I may be wrong about this, but I believe I'm the only person that Josie's Cabaret and Juice Joint ever pulled a show on. They said it was because I did not get enough reservations, but that's obviously not the case since I attended a number of shows there, running shows, where I was one of the two or three audience members. The audience numbers for *Go* were well below the space's average for such kinds of shows, but they had steadily increased day after day. I've talked to colleagues who had more dismal audiences but were still allowed to finished their run.

The experience of *Go* in San Francisco was a difficult one. It was a poke in the eye. Hell, it was repeated pokings everywhere on my body. The marketing of the show also made audiences expect a very different kind of performance, something more theatrical, or at least something funnier or empowering, certainly not the tripe they were subjected to.

Hard-worn lessons were learned. But I was never allowed to work at Josie's again.

Still, Josie's was a great space, and they presented a lot of good work and gave a lot of artists in the germinal stage of their careers a boost. Sadly, Josie's fell prey to the whims of The City's economy and its fickle paying audiences. The dysfunc-

Attack of the Man-Eating Lotus Blossoms

tional inner-workings of the space, fueled by alcohol, and felled by illness, squabbles, and burn-out finally finished poor Josie's off. A trendy noodle house moved in and that, as they as, was that.

I'm still very fond of the writing in *Go*. Parts of it were incorporated into *Infinite Read* [www.queerculturalcenter.org/Justin/], a web-art commission by the San Francisco Queer Cultural Center in 2000.

***

(Four large mason jars, each containing a stuffed animal pickling in either vinegar or pickle juice, are onstage. There is a small television downstage center. If possible, the floor of the stage should be covered in dunes of rock salt. Also, if possible, the performer should be dressed in a bear suit, or any plush animal costume, minus the head, of course.

The sound of movie-projector reels clacking. The closing lines of the movie The World of Suzie Wong *are heard:*
　　Robert: Suzie, please, will you marry me?
　　Suzie: Robert, I stay with you until you say, "Suzie, you go."
The sound of the film reels abruptly ends in a nails-on-the-blackboard screech.)

SLIDE:

> **Suzie Wong, as worn by Justin Chin, Performance Artist. $10.00.**

SUZIE WONG: He said Go. So here I am, stuck in Anytown U.S.A., finally able to speak, read, and write English correctly and still, my life is one goddam tragic TV melodrama movie-of-the-week. HOOKER WITH QUINTESSENTIAL HEART OF GOLD DUMPED FOR LITTLE THAI BOY.

(The television suddenly pops on. It is playing The World of Suzie

Justin Chin

Wong. *There is no sound and the picture is fuzzy, much like how scrambled cable channels appear or how copy-protected tapes reproduce. At unexpected points, the movie might scroll forward or backward, jump sequences, speed up or slow down so much that it is almost a frame-by-frame showing.*

> I have every reason to be bitter. Once I heard a poem that said, "Bitterness is a root/ incriminating, evil/ free for all to see." So I like to hide my bitterness in a nice story. I'm going to tell you a story. This is a story about my life. I've absolutely no reason to tell you this story except that I want to. This story about my life may not even be true. Everything I tell you will either be a truth or such a damn lie. In either case, I'll tell you whether to believe me or not, and whether you do or not, will be entirely up to you. But you must always remember that there's a lot of truth in lies and a lot of lies in truths.

SLIDE:

> Truth, as worn by Authenticity. $6.99.

> For those of you who have tuned in at this point, sucked into this moment of THE STORY, let me try to place you into where we all are. Me: I am Suzie Wong. You are Suzie Wong. He/She/It is Suzie Wong. You are/They are/We are Suzie Wong. I met Mr. Robert Lomax on a ferry to Hong Kong. He had disposed of his life as a banker to be an artist in Hong Kong. We meet. We exchange witty yet charmingly Oriental banter. We're mutually smitten in some bizarre way. We go through angst about our lives and our professions, real or imagined. We break up because of the angst of our lives and our professions, real or imagined. I lose my child in a freak monsoon flood (the roof fell in on his little bastard mulatto head). He comforts me and helps me bury my child. We fall in love again. We marry. (In the book, I get some bizarre blood disease and he gives me a blood transfusion; in the flick, we just marry. The difference in the construction is how light feeds your eye.)

Attack of the Man-Eating Lotus Blossoms

Our lives. Our life...wasn't always like that. It used to be so good. I believed that he loved me. I believed anything he said, any sentence that was constructed with the word "love" in it.

SLIDE:

> Idiosyncrasy, as worn by Duplicity. $3.99.
> Shoes by Traditionalism. $5.99.
> Hair & Makeup by Approval.

After I said that I would be his forever, we left for Bangkok. Robert wanted to take me far away from the Nam Kok, the wrenching house of prostitution that I called Home. "Take me away from all the evils, away from all the sailors that knew me, away from my reputation, away from my friends, away from everything that I know as my world, my man." From the moment we got on board that steamship, he was all that was to be my world. I've always liked traveling by water. I like the feeling of floating. It's funny how water brought me to this point: the rains, the floods, and now it's still with me.

Bangkok wasn't all that different, actually. Robert's paintings were beginning to sell in London. His paintings of me. Me lying on his bed. Me on the veranda holding an apple. Me fishing. Me in silk.

SLIDE:

> History, as worn by Personality. $4.95.

But Bangkok, it all seemed like being in Hong Kong all again, except for the language and the food. Robert liked Bangkok, he liked Thailand. He liked all the culture, the pristine beauty, he said. The only reason Bangkok and all of Thailand was left to its culture and pristine beauty was because the French, the Dutch, and the English decided that it was to be a buffer zone between their properties. A

Club Med for them to shake all their troubles away. And even then, the edges were being rubbed raw. There was a war going on, you see. How so inconsiderate it all was.

I read somewhere that some people who watch too much TV sometimes develop this form of psychosis that makes them unable to differentiate between what is on their screens and what is reality. I think that's really strange. I think it's scary that a person can replace *Bewitched* and a war in his head, or diseases and starvation with *Dynasty*, and not know which one can be turned off and which one will kill you right off.

This was supposed to be our romantic honeymoon led into newlywed life, where we were supposed to be deliriously happy. But every time I go to the markets to buy food for our meals, there is talk, new talk about this village blown up, hundreds of people killed. Some say the Americans came in blasting with tanks, some say it was the Viet Cong's cold-blooded murdering. Whichever one, it still makes me scared. I keep dreaming that one day I might be in that village when someone who doesn't know me or care to know me simply kills me.

Robert believes in the good of military intervention. He says that that is the only thing that can be done to save anyone now, *someone has to be sacrificed*, he says, stroking my hair.

But what if that somebody is me? I say. He strokes my hair, kisses the back of my neck and says, Never, it'll never happen. I'll be the first one to save you. I'll find someone else for the sacrifice.

SLIDE:

> **Formal Experience, as worn by Lived Experience.**
> **$3.99/minute. 18 and over only, please.**

THE BOY: You'd be surprised at what passes for a relationship around here.

(*Pulls two of the stuffed animals out of their jars and uses them to*

Attack of the Man-Eating Lotus Blossoms

illustrate the story. Do not wring; the stuffed animals should be dripping fluids.)

Take the case of this guy I know. THE TRAGIC TEENAGER says he's in a relationship with THE GERMAN. THE TRAGIC TEENAGER meets THE GERMAN during the man's vacation, fucked for a week and then they're both pledging undying love in heavily scented letters every week. Fake Giorgio. THE TRAGIC TEENAGER bursts into the coffee shop every week like clockwork, clutching THE GERMAN's letters in his hand, all sent Poste Restante, and hysterically delirious, crying about how much he misses THE GERMAN. Every month or so, THE GERMAN sends pictures of himself and his family: wife and three kids plus dog and picnic table taken at some Oktoberfest a year ago. THE TRAGIC TEENAGER cuts the wife and kids out of the picture and pastes THE GERMAN and THE DOG and picnic table over this photo of himself at the beach. Oktoberfest at Phuket: A Portrait of True Love as Collage. Then THE TRAGIC TEENAGER would run off and write his love letter, complete with alluring photo reminder, all sent off in an envelope Poste Restante.

There're all these kids who maintain these relationships with these foreigners from all over the world who maybe show up again, maybe never. But when they do, you can bet they've got a warm place to sleep, a hot meal on a tray, and a guaranteed hot fuck with even more pledges of undying love. And the latter is what makes it all tick, isn't it. The relationship as YMCA Brothel.

There're all these guys that are in relationships with men who left so long ago and have never returned that the letters back and forth professing undying love, promises to be together again, and reminiscences of the past fuck past swoon past romance become as mechanical as programming the VCR. But as long as that one parcel every birthday, every Christmas goes back and forth Poste Restante then everything is as beautiful as any Whitney Houston ballad on her first album.

Justin Chin

But who am I to speak, because here I am: me with Mr. Robert Lomax. Do we have a relationship? He says, Yes. I say, You'd be surprised at what passes for a relationship around here these days.

SLIDE:

> **Currency, as worn by Self-Pity. Free.**

SUZIE WONG: You'd be surprised at what passes for love these days.

(Pulls one of the stuffed animals out of its jar. It is a very Cabbage Patch-like doll, but much cheaper. Used to animate the story, the doll is held at arms length horizontally and is slowly rotated face-up to face-down continually. It too should be dripping fluid.)

There's this girl I know. I met her one day at a bar. THE GILDED VIRGIN HOOKER is sweet, attractive, but still kind of plain because of all the makeup and teased hair. We sit at the bar and kill time before her next date. She has one special boyfriend, she tells me. She shows me the picture of him. A nice-looking GI boy. He's standing in front of a tank with his friends. I know which one he is without her telling me because there is a round black-marker-pen circle around one of the boys. He's going to come back real soon, she says.

For a brief flash, I would have been really sad for her thinking that she would be thinking about him coming back. THE GILDED VIRGIN HOOKER spending her nights with temporary boyfriends and sleeping with the gray teddy bear he gave her. But for one brief flash, I realize that it is a useless endeavor to be sad for anyone.

One day, we're sitting on the front steps talking and THE GOOD SOLDIER shows up. He stands very still at the end of the street, so still that we almost don't see him. But when someone is standing at the end of street, standing still, something happens to the flow of light and you

Attack of the Man-Eating Lotus Blossoms

notice. THE GILDED VIRGIN HOOKER looks up and cries a sound that sounds like a small animal being squished by a truck. THE GOOD SOLDIER and THE GILDED VIRGIN HOOKER run to each other, some melodramatic moment in a love story. You almost expect the entire scene to flicker in slow motion, frame by frame. So THE GOOD SOLDIER has returned to save THE GILDED VIRGIN HOOKER, and THE GILDED VIRGIN HOOKER has stayed THE GILDED VIRGIN HOOKER for THE GOOD SOLDIER. Even then, such consistency is rare.

SLIDE:

> **Formalism, as worn by Pleasure. $7.99.**
> **Fragrance: Essence of Democracy.**

Two weeks later, THE GILDED VIRGIN HOOKER tells me that THE GOOD SOLDIER has gone AWOL. THE GILDED VIRGIN HOOKER doesn't grasp the meaning nor the severity of the acronym. I tell her that all this means she gets to keep him real safe from anyone who wants to hurt him, she gets to keep him for good, for as long as either of the lovers want.

Two days later, THE GILDED VIRGIN HOOKER comes to me crying. She doesn't want THE GOOD SOLDIER anymore. In between her sobbing, she tells me that THE GOOD SOLDIER is in torment in her bed. "He is dreaming," she says. In that vestige of rapid eye movements, THE GOOD SOLDIER is either killing someone who looks like THE GILDED VIRGIN HOOKER while she is cooking lunch or is being killed by someone who looks like THE GILDED VIRGIN HOOKER while he is cooking lunch.

In one dream, the kitchen is green-tiled, the dish is eggs and ham, the knife used for the act is blue-bladed with a gray handle. In the other dream, the kitchen is orange linoleum, the dish is peanut meatloaf, the knife used for the act is pink-bladed with a white handle. In either case, the blood from the lover's neck is red.

Justin Chin

The dream is not the problem, of course, and THE GILDED VIRGIN HOOKER and THE GOOD SOLDIER know that. It's the act of killing in the dream that's the problem. It's the most intimate act of murder, the slicing of throats, you see. If the act was sheer shelling, blowing up the damn house containing the body, poisoning, all this relationship trauma wouldn't be happening. But the slicing of a throat needs a degree of intimacy that is scary.

THE GOOD SOLDIER is telling THE GILDED VIRGIN HOOKER all this like any good lover should/would. And suddenly, the happiest place in their world, the soft comfy bed where so many promises were made, secrets shared, body language explained, and kisses traded in passionate declarations of love has become the ugliest thing in the world. But are a war and a poor shell-shocked GI the only things necessary to wreck a good bed?

So THE GILDED VIRGIN HOOKER doesn't want THE GOOD SOLDIER anymore, but this isn't the RSPCA, is it?

(Each time during The Chorus, the performer moves in front of the television. The only light onstage comes from the television screen, and the performer is reduced to a silhouette in front of it. Staring at the movie, beginning as a casual onlooker then slowing turning into an awed spectator, the performer nervously reaches out to touch the screen, then apprehensively pokes at the figures on screen.)

THE CHORUS:
>Once we had three Gods
>That appeared to us
>Looking for virtue.
>We gave them shelter
>And they called us Good.
>So now, we are cursed
>With the great power,
>The most thankless gift,
>Of being able
>To recognize at
>One simple glance,
>One fleeting look,
>The canon of Gods

Attack of the Man-Eating Lotus Blossoms

That may appear
Before humans.
It has been long known
That devils walk the world
Looking for evil
Among the living.
And angels walk too,
But only looking
For utter goodness
And sheer virtue.
Now, there are few angels
That walk, instead,
The Gods themselves
Must do the work.
There are many rumors
Why the Gods have come
To replace the angels.
Some say, it is due to
Cutbacks in heaven's budget.
Others say it's because
The amount of evil
Has increased tenfold.
Still others say that
There has been too much
Dying in the last
Few decades & that
The angels are too sad,
Too tired, too depressed,
Too cynical,
Too suicidal,
To be much good
Anymore.

Whatever the reason,
It is our job to introduce
The major Gods that
You may chance across.
It is important
To know these Gods
So that you do not
Simply walk by them.

Justin Chin

It is a regretful act
To walk by a God
Without even knowing it.
Many people make
The mistake of thinking
That Gods are beautiful
Or male. But no,
They are anything,
Anyone. You can't be sure.
So please listen to us.

Now let us introduce to you,
The first God:

The God of Water. Cannot be seen, unlike most of the other Gods. This one is like vapor. The God of Water lives in everything that is water, in everything that is wet. It is the most important thing in the world because water is in all food, it grows all plants and quenches the thirst of all animals. The God of Water is the most forceful when found on the human body. On a hot day, you summon it up and it drenches you in a cool trickle of sweat down your neck. When you are excited or scared, it is summoned as a coldness and chills your bones so that the external world will always be warmer to you. The God of Water is the one who allows you to drown.

But the God of Water is most powerful when it is called up between two bodies. When the space between the flesh heats up because they are pressed against each other, the heat calls up a wetness and the God is called and it is the most serene state it will ever want to be in.

Next is the God of War:

The God of War does not only control wars. It also controls anger and rage. It is, again, like the God of Diseases and Epidemics, a good God even though it passes emotions that are ugly and make people hurt. The God of War wears a seamless robe of two colors and carries a map painted with saffron oil, a compass, a bucket of cinders, and a large talking fish. This too is a secretive God and not much is

Attack of the Man-Eating Lotus Blossoms

known of how this God works. All you need to know is that it is needed and that when summoned, it can be most powerful. This God always appears in loud noise. This God travels faster than the speed of the invisible particles that shoot out of your nose when you sneeze or your mouth when you are shouting.

SLIDE:

> **Intimation, as worn by Some Really Pissed-Off Folks. $15.95.**

(The sound of movie-projector reels clacking. Dialogue from the scene in the movie The World of Suzie Wong *— the part where Suzie Wong lyingly brags to the other bar-girls that Robert has hit her out of jealously — is heard.*

Gwenny: Suzie! What happened!

Suzie: Oh nothing. That Robert, I tell you, he so crazy mad about me he give me a good beating because he think I go with another man.

Minnie: Robert did that?

Suzie: I tell you. He's crazy mad about me. He so jealous. He so in love with me. I go now. See you tomorrow, girls. Too bad you don't have a good man beat you too.)

SLIDE:

> **Grammar, as worn by Enunciation. Prices vary on models and options. "We Offer First Time Buyer Plan!" Finance rates as low as 6.5% APR. All prices plus tax, lic., doc. fees and dealer installed options. Leases excluded. Subject to credit approval. APR on approved credit only. Subject to price changes. SALE ENDS SOON!!**

SUZIE WONG: Robert and me. Robert and I. Who gives a flying fuck which is grammatically correct anymore.

Did I ever love Robert? That's an easy one. Yes, I did. I

used to be so scared that I would lose him. I used to be so scared that he would suddenly wake up one day and find me hideous and he would leave me. Or he would find someone else more wonderful. Eventually, he did. But by then, I knew it was coming and by then, I didn't care anymore. You always know when a relationship is screeching to an end.

Did I ever love Robert? That's an easy one. Once a journalist asked me to describe what I loved about Robert. Or rather the question was to describe what it was like to be in love. And I interpreted the question as it applied to Robert because it was he who I was in love with at that time. I should have seen the grammatical trap, but I didn't.

The journalists pushed his tape-recorder microphone toward me and I said, in a full complete sentence like a practice language tape, "What I love about Robert is that he loves me." That sounds like such an incredibly simple-minded answer, but that was all I could think of then. Perhaps there was a grain of truth in it, perhaps it was what I thought I would always say when asked such a question, perhaps.

Now. Do I love Robert? Or do I still love Robert? That's an easy one too.

SLIDE:

> **Essentialism, as worn by Self-Deprecation. $8.99. Accessories created by Karmic Co-Dependence.**

THE BOY: What is a relationship anyway? It can be one of any number of definitions, I guess.

(Produces a stack of cue cards out of nowhere and reads the questions off them, tossing each card with a great flourish.)

Can a foreigner who loves a man because of his culture also love the man himself? Would that foreigner love that man if the man were to suddenly, without warning, give

Attack of the Man-Eating Lotus Blossoms

up his culture and assimilate into another? What if the man comes from a hybrid culture, an amalgamation of two or more, and is wholly undefined except for that man's reality? Can a foreigner who loves a man because he thinks the man will respond and behave according to some cultivated expectations and prejudices still love the man if those expectations and prejudices did not ever occur? Would the foreigner even want to love such a man in the first place? Can a foreigner who looks at a man of a particular culture with fetishistic gaze be able to truly love that man? Would it then be the man or the obsession? Can a foreigner who loves a man in spite of his culture also love the man because of his culture?

Don't look at me like I have any answers that might interest you. They're just questions. And I'm just some kid hoping that each episode of hot Fabio-romance is the one. I'm not some bloody anthro-sociologist with all the damn answers footnoted and tagged so neatly you could fuck and fold. Can anyone really answer these damn questions anyway?

And do they really matter? THE TRAGIC TEENAGER doesn't think so. Then again, he doesn't know where and when to begin asking. That's what I share with him.

(This time in front of the television, the performer is an invested witness. The performer sits closer to the television and unhesitatingly touches the screen, trying to caress and fondle, sometimes even trying to grab, the figures that appear onscreen.)

THE CHORUS: Hear us now:
  Let the roll of Gods
  Continue:

The God of Mercy is an easy God. This God is so gentle and docile, it is almost like a petting zoo. The God of Mercy is best friends with the God of War and the God of Diseases. It's like they say, opposites attract. This God tries to soothe. Rather like a calamine lotion of the soul. The God of Mercy most likes to manifest itself in a gentle kiss.

This God cannot be summoned, it will come and go as it pleases. It is overworked.

Also overworked is the God of Exorcisms. This God is clothed in overalls and the brightest white robes even though it does the most dirty work of any God. This God appears suddenly and never stays for long. Its main job is to purge the nastiest bits out of one's body. It does this by gouging out the eyes of demons that plague the body and eating them.

The Exorcism of Snobbery and Decay
A certain Emperor was sprinkled with the spores of a dreadful illness by the God of Diseases. On his sickbed, in a sweat where even the God of Water had deserted him, the Emperor saw a small demon dancing in his room. The demon had a fuzzed face like a monkey, was in his bare feet, and had his shoes tied around his neck. Attached to the demon's head was a soft cap of many colors. The demon jumped up on the bed and danced on the Emperor's belly, mocking the Emperor in a song. The Emperor indignantly cried, "Who are you?" "I am the Demon of Snobbery and Decay," the little demon replied. "With Snobbery, you need not look at others and so you can become the most beautiful and with Decay you can turn the healthy into nothing but rot." The Emperor was angry with such an arrogant reply and at that moment, the God of Exorcism appeared, poked the demon's eyes out and ate them in one gulp. The Emperor woke in a start and realized that his illness was gone.

The Exorcism of Insignificance and Devastation
A certain Emperor was sprinkled with the spores of a dreadful illness by the God of Diseases. On his sickbed, in a sweat where even the God of Water had deserted him, the Emperor saw a small demon dancing in his room. The demon looked like a small child with big ears and large feet. The demon was wearing one shoe on his left foot and a sandal on his right. He had bloodshot eyes that he did not bother to hide, and his breath smelled like wet grass. He was dancing on the Emperor's legs. "Who are you,

Attack of the Man-Eating Lotus Blossoms

why are you tormenting me?" the Emperor cried. "I am the demon of Insignificance and Devastation," the demon replied. "With Insignificance, you become so hollow that you can fly; with Devastation, you can turn the healthy into nothing but rot!" The Emperor was angered at the vapidity and the arrogance of this reply but was unable to do anything as the demon had started hacking at the Emperor's knees with a small hatchet. Suddenly, the God of Exorcism appeared, poked out the bloodshot eyes of the demon, dipped them in the demon's blood, and ate them one by one. The Emperor then woke with a start and his illness was floating above him like a haze of cannabis smoke.

The God of Exorcisms was originally a court-artist of the Emperor. He wrote the most beautiful essays and poems, but the Emperor did not want to listen to them because this court-artist was not beautiful. The Emperor had no place for any ugly court-artists. But the ugly court-artist still loved the Emperor. To prove this, the ugly court-artist wrote an epic love poem for the Emperor, but still the Emperor put on his Walkman, refused to listen, and so the court-artist killed himself on the steps of the Imperial Palace. The Emperor, racked with guilt, ordered an imperial funeral for the ugly man. From then on, because of the way he died, the ugly court-artist became the God of Exorcisms.

SLIDE:

> **Special Combo Meal Deal: Homosexuality, Ethnicity + Large Fries & Medium Soft Drink. $4.95. NO SUBSTITUTIONS PLEASE. Super Size: 69¢. Special Disney Toy OR Fun Straw: 99¢.**

THE BOY: Robert has befriended THE EVERSMILING THAI BOY. Robert has been speaking about smiles a lot lately. He has become quite enamored of the mythical, legendary Thai smile. "These people are so serene, so happy," he tells me. "They always greet you with a smile, even strangers, but for the familiar, it's even better."

It's not the first time I've heard this. People from all around the world have mentioned the Thai capacity for smiling. It's even in the travel brochure, the travel posters, the travel ads: come halfway around the world and let a whole damn nation of Third World natives smile at you, Colgate white. But there's smiles and there's grins. One is the cruel sister to the other, one's the evil cousin to the smirk, it takes a connoisseur of smiles to tell them apart.

So dear Robert has befriended THE EVERSMILING THAI BOY. One day, Robert comes home from the market with a bag of mangosteens; it's a good score, there're out of season at this time. He wants to bring some over to THE EVERSMILING THAI BOY, immediately. He carefully transfers the purple fruits to a clear red plastic bag that once held broken china plates and leaves from THE EVERSMILING THAI BOY's house; he wants to see the delighted smile on the boy's face, he wants to capture that smile in his mind, he wants to remember that smile on his new canvas.

He meets THE EVERSMILING THAI BOY. THE EVERSMILING THAI BOY is smiling but not smiling as Robert remembers. Why? inquires Robert. He is genuinely concerned. THE EVERSMILING THAI BOY tells Robert that he has since discovered that life is a cycle of sufferings. Robert gives THE EVERSMILING THAI BOY the mangosteens. THE EVERSMILING THAI BOY smiles but not the smile that Robert remembers again. Robert is disappointed. Robert tries to reassure THE EVER-SMILING THAI BOY that life would be much better if one makes an effort to see that it is. Robert demands that THE EVERSMILING THAI BOY smile; that will make life a lot happier and brighter if you smile; a smile a day keeps sadness at bay. THE EVERSMILING THAI BOY says that he is smiling, that he is smiling like he always smiles. Robert is disappointed. Robert is grumpy the whole day.

Attack of the Man-Eating Lotus Blossoms

SLIDE:

> **Incarnadine, as worn by Cynicism. $4.95. Accessories by Affirmation. Hair and Makeup by Catharticism.**

THE BOY: Mr. Robert Lomax says he loves me very much. He shows me pictures of his ex-wife when they were together in Bangkok more than twenty years ago. He's divorced now and she is somewhere in America, he says. Mr. Robert Lomax is a painter. He wants to paint me, but I tell him that I don't want to be painted. He says, Paint to draw a picture of you. He thinks that I think that he wants to *paint* me. I tell him I know what the fuck he means, and he laughs.

(The performer adopts a slouchy hunched stance, leaning more and more into it as the monologue progresses and as the speech's pace increases and becomes more emphatic. By the end of this monologue, the performer is almost curled into an armadillo-like ball but still standing.)

He likes everything about my cultures, he says. "The people, the places, the atmosphere is just so nice...I mean, it's just so different, so easy-going and open and friendly, yea, that's right, friendly...and the people are so beautiful, not like model beautiful, though so many are, but their souls...their hearts, it's that that counts, right? But you, you are beautiful both inside and outside..." He says things like that a lot as if he's trying to convince himself instead of me.

My friend says that it might be senility setting in, "The poor man is obviously shell-shocked from his divorce, his shitty has-been career, and his pathetic attempts to overcome his impotence."

Mr. Robert Lomax is in his sixties. He doesn't want to tell me his real age, but one day when he went out to buy lunch, I looked at his passport. He says it really doesn't matter, and he's right, really, because it doesn't. Except when he leans back in his easy chair, makes me put my head on his lap, rolls his eyes back in some tantric state

37

between nirvana and psychoneurosis, and starts to tell me about this war and that war, the moon landing, the assassination of JFK, and how the OPEC oil crisis was the pivotal point in changing America's standing as the world leader.

He doesn't ever get hard anymore, so hanging out with him is quite easy. He likes it nice and easy. It's not his age, I know that; I've been with very handsome men much older than him who can still fuck like they're eighteen but with much more patience, and they can still tear my ass up in the process.

Mr. Robert Lomax says he loves me. That he can't live without me. That he has never ever loved anyone like he loves me.

You'd be surprised at what passes for love these days.

The worst thing that ever happened to the word "love" and the "concept" of it is the modern sentimental ballad. Suddenly, *true* rhymes with *blue* and *I love you* and everything else spirals in some Brownian motion from there. Fabulous. And if you can hold that one note at the end, the big *Star Search-Eurovision-Talenttime* finish, baby you got it made.

Why am I with Mr. Robert Lomax?

Why not? You'd be surprised at what passes for love these days.

(Now, the performer has turned into a fixated gawker. The performer's interactions with the figures onscreen are now boldly sexual, even a little crude. This behavior get progressively more physical until the performer is trying to lick, trying to seriously tongue, every character than appears onscreen.)

THE CHORUS: Let us introduce
   To you good people:
   The last God you need to know.
   This is the God of Earth and Fire. This is also known as the God of Burials. This God is a very big and strong spirit

Attack of the Man-Eating Lotus Blossoms

with strong arms and muscular shoulders and back. It is dressed in blue and carries a metal stake in one hand and a shovel in the other. The God of Earth and Fire is also in charge of cremating and burying those its colleagues, the God of War and the God of Diseases, have decimated. The God of Earth and Fire keeps a log of all it has burnt and buried and says their names every night before going to rest. The God of Earth and Fire is a very sad God. It cries a lot but never lets anyone see it cry. We only know it cries because of the moss on gravestones.

They say that
To be forewarned
Is to be forearmed.
But the good people,
The virtuous, those
Who try too hard to be,
Live to be far
Far too old and hungry
For some big want.
Can anyone blame anyone?

There, these are five
Gods that you may chance
Across. There are much
Much more, lurking
About, walking and
Strolling among all
Of the world but these
Five, you must know.
Why, Why,
Why are you telling us
All this, you cry? Why
Have you broken though
The membranes of our comfort
And our ignorance?
Now we will surely
Be looking out for Gods
To be gracious to.
Did we not have enough
Trouble looking out

Justin Chin

For devils to avoid!
Now how can anyone
Walk down the street
To buy a block of ice
Or salt
And not be paranoid
That we may tread
On the toes of some
Powerful God who
May sprinkle disaster
On us and our families?

Oh, what is a person to do?
Oh, why must we live
With the weight of such
Sorrow?

SLIDE:

> **Possibility, as worn by Consensualism. $5.99.
> Hair by Validity; Makeup by Acquiescence™
> ("Hypoallergenic & not tested on animals")**

SUZIE WONG: One day, Robert comes to me and says, "Suzie, you don't know what tenderness is, all you know is sex." It is the middle of the afternoon and I am sitting on the veranda reading a magazine. "It's not the same thing, you know, you think it is, you have been brought up to think it is, but it isn't. Perhaps it's your native language, it doesn't have the delicate complexities and layerings of the English language." I want to teach you what tenderness is, he declares.

(Pulls the remaining stuffed animal out of its jar. Holding the stuffed toy in one hand and a knife or a barbecue fork in the other, the performer stabs or pokes the stuffed toy. Already drippy, each poke nonetheless makes the stuffed toy spew more fluids. The performer then skewers the stuffed animal posteriorly on the knife or the barbecue fork and uses it as a stick puppet.)

Attack of the Man-Eating Lotus Blossoms

ROBERT'S LESSON ON HOW TO BE TENDER
To be tender, you must not confuse it with weakness or sympathy. To be tender you must be meek yet strong. One of the meanings of tender is to offer, to give, to tender. To tender is tender.

The best place to start learning how to be tender is in the bedroom. When this is achieved, you may move to the bathroom, then the kitchen, following that, the living and/or dining rooms, and lastly, any adjoining external spaces such as balconies, verandas, and car porches.

Tenderness can be shown while having sex, preparing meals, washing the car, dry-walling, marketing, open-heart surgery, kidney transplants, balancing the checkbook, and even washing dishes.

To be tender, face the object that is to receive the tender and treat it as if it were a jeweled heirloom feather made of cobwebs encrusted with dust. Cobwebs are known to be the strongest thread of its diameter, but a slight careless brush will snap them, sending spiders, insect meals, and dust in all directions.

Robert has finished a new painting. The canvas is resting on his easel. I look at the painting. It is in his usual naturalistic style. The painting is a portrait of a person, dressed in a black robe sitting in front of a large house, smiling *Mona Lisa* serene. SO serene she should be holding a load of enriched white bread.

Who is this? I ask him.

He looks surprised. It's you, he says. Don't you recognize yourself? I've painted dozens of portraits of you.

I look at the picture again. It is not my smile. It is someone else's smile. I don't smile like that. I never have.

SLIDE:

Approximation, as worn by A Performance Artist That Has Yet to Take His Clothes Off in Any of His Performances, If Only Because He Feels Really Really Flabby. $8.95.

Justin Chin

(From here on till the end, the piece is performed andante, a bit melancholic perhaps, even sweetly plaintive.)

THE BOY: There are some places where dogs are afraid to bark. If a dog barks at night and no dog barks back in conversation, then the dog has seen a ghost, a spirit.

I am in dire need of tenderness, Robert declares one day. He looks at me as if I am supposed to do something about his dire need. All my life, I am in dire need of tenderness and I have found it with you, he declares. He smiles and places his head in my lap.

Woof.

Mr. Robert Lomax is sleeping. He is sleeping in my bed. It is early morning. I am sitting on the veranda looking out into the city. Mr. Robert Lomax has given his heart to me. I don't know what to do with it. He entreats me to be tender with it, thought I have no idea what I have to do to achieve that. There has to be more choices than *love* and *tender*. This I do know for sure: some men will be loved all their lives and some men will never be loved all their lives. You know very early on which one you will be. Neither one nor the other is good nor bad, they just are. I discovered very early on which one I was to be, and I am enduring it.

Woof.

There are tourists and there are travelers. Both will go the distance, both want to see as much as possible, both are looking for adventure, both are looking for something new, both are looking for the real thing, both are willing to pay for the real thing; but one will eventually long for some semblance of home, one is already home.

And Robert? And Robert keeps asking for transfers for one more ride.

Woof.

Attack of the Man-Eating Lotus Blossoms

SLIDE:

> Justin Chin, as worn by Identity, Bugbear. $9.99.
> Accessories: Model's own.

(The sound of movie-projector reels clacking. The closing lines of the movie The World of Suzie Wong *are heard. But this time, these lines repeat in irregular loops. The clacking segues into an ethereal soundscape of shrieks, screams, yelps, and wailing; however, these are in no way frightful or threatening sounds, in fact, they are strangely musical and symphonious. The closing lines are still looping.*
Robert: Suzie, please, will you marry me?
Suzie: Robert, I stay with you until you say, "Suzie, you go."
Small bits of sentimental love songs — Linda Ronstadt's version of "I Will Always Love You," Tom Jones' "It's Not Unusual," power ballads from the '80s — pop out through all of this, as if someone was turning the dial on a radio and passing various stations.)

SUZIE WONG: There are some people who will be loved throughout their lives and there are some people who will be unloved throughout their lives. You discover very early on in life which one you'll be. Then you can either fight it like a champion boxer until you're damaged or you can take it face on. Penelope Pitstop, unsaved by The Anthill Mob, run over by the train, sawed in half by the timber saw. There's nothing wrong with either, actually. It's just the way some folks choose to live. Nothing to do with blessings or curses, so don't bother your saints, your gods, and your deities; don't bother with incantations, charms, and magic. Don't bother at all.

Something very strange happened two weeks after they dropped the bomb on Nagasaki. One day, quite suddenly, irises started to sprout and bloom out of the ripped soil. Normally, the bulbs would have remained dormant until the appropriate season, but perhaps due to the heat, the radiation, and the trauma to the earth, the bulbs pushed out of the earth and within days bloomed into their usual lush blues and yellows. They didn't know better. They probably thought that it was time, and they stuck their little buds out into the air only to find people dead, dying, burnt, ill, crippled, homeless, and too shell-shocked to care about flowers blooming out of season in poisoned ground.

> *Robert: Suzie, please, will you marry me?*
> *Suzie: Robert, I stay with you until you say, "Suzie, you go."*

Where are we in THE STORY. The true/false STORY of my life with Mr. Robert Lomax. There are holes obviously. Big holes you could trip and fall into like some Jerry Lewis slapstick comedy. Big holes like an electron pushed to an outer orbital, creating a space for something to fall in. Waiting for something to fall in and fill it.

Robert is gone. The war around me has changed, a silly game of musical chairs. When the music stops, and the extra chair is whisked away, and another whisked away, until the last one is left standing as the world stares at THE UNFORTUNATE ONE who wasn't fast enough to wriggle their buttocks onto the last remaining seat.

> *Robert: Suzie, please, will you marry me?*
> *Suzie: Robert, I stay with you until you say, "Suzie, you go."*

Robert is gone and he never sacrificed anything for me as he promised. All I'm looking for is one good sacrifice. And I got it, too.

Some lies are the subversion of experience, the prized monster in a freak show.

> *Robert: Suzie, please, will you marry me?*
> *Suzie: Robert, I stay with you until you say, "Suzie, you go."*

The big gaping hole that you fell in is the exquisite sacrifice. Believe everything I tell you even as I tell you that there are no such things as a True Story.
   "How many holes does it take to fill the Royal Albert Hall?"

> *Robert: Suzie, please, will you marry me?*

Attack of the Man-Eating Lotus Blossoms

Suzie: Robert, I stay with you until you say, "Suzie, you go."

I invent. I invent. I invent and we're back in THE STORY searching for the sacrifice as the music starts again. Ten chairs laid out waiting for THE NEXT UNFORTUNATE ONE.

I am as old as my mother's blood and I am still full of holes.

(The loop of movie dialogue has progressively gotten quieter and quieter but in such small decrements that one hardly notices it fading out. It can still be heard, but seems like an echo. The screams and shrieks seem to have gotten quieter too, but they only seem that way because they are being played backward. The bits of pop songs now linger in slightly longer snatches.
    This polyphony continues even after the lights have very slowly faded to black, and then it too fades away.)

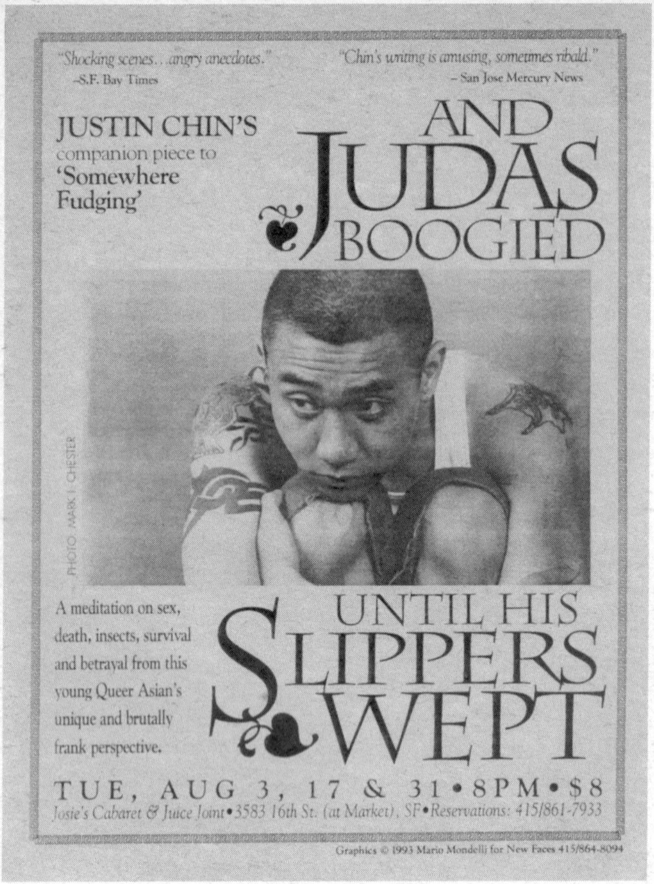

"Shocking scenes... angry anecdotes."
–S.F. Bay Times
"Chin's writing is amusing, sometimes ribald."
– San Jose Mercury News
JUSTIN CHIN'S
companion piece to
'Somewhere Fudging'
AND JUDAS BOOGIED
PHOTO: MARK I. CHESTER
A meditation on sex, death, insects, survival and betrayal from this young Queer Asian's unique and brutally frank perspective.
UNTIL HIS SLIPPERS WEPT
TUE, AUG 3, 17 & 31 • 8PM • $8
Josie's Cabaret & Juice Joint • 3583 16th St. (at Market), SF • Reservations: 415/861-7933
Graphics © 1993 Mario Mondelli for New Faces 415/864-8094

And Judas Boogied Until His Slippers Wept
(1993-1996)

Judas... is actually the second performance work I created.

The first was *Somewhere Fudging*, a performance monologue in the character of a young Asian guy who works as a house cleaner and how he sorts through life and love, dating and the scene in San Francisco in the early '90s. The show was decidedly GenX and referenced a lot of '70s and '80s pop culture, and also featured elaborate fantasy sequences with Connie Chung and Miss Saigon, a fan letter to George Takei, trips to rice bars, gay bars, a Queer Nation Kiss-In, and a men's encounter weekend, and the "So You Think You're a Rice Queen" quiz. And no, it was *not* autobiographical.

The work hasn't aged very well, and when I look at it now, I feel a slight bit of embarrassment tinged with nostalgia. Did I really used to write and think like this? *What was I thinking?* I ask myself. I'm sure a lot of the sentiments contained in the piece still hold true for many people — the search for love and belonging will endlessly play itself out till the end of humankind, and the inane and often skin-crawling comments that white men with a penchant for Asian men used to say then are still being said now — but there are much better ways of writing it out, and performing it out.

Somewhere Fudging is largely responsible, however, for the "Angry Gay Asian" tag that I seem to have been tarred with. A charge that totally confounds and amuses my best friends and my family.

I do believe the "angry" accusation is usually made to dismiss a person's opinions wholesale, a way of not having to take them seriously, or at all, since it's just "emotional," a hissy fit. It's used quite liberally with art by people of color, art with a feminist thrust, and political art that challenges the dominant mode. The ploy is a good one in that it's easily parroted, and if done often enough or emphatically enough, will be adopted by others who are too lethargic or unmotivated to think for themselves. For those whose opinion of you, for whatever reason, is already brimming with acrimony and venom, the accusation is a gift.

Admittedly, some audiences' witnessing of anger is actually that, but they perhaps don't recognize that there is a difference too between anger and a performed anger, the latter being an examination or a critique of the former or its sources. And then there is rage, which is so much more sensible and preferable for political purposes.

As the earliest work represented in this collection, *Judas...* feels like it's encased in amber, freeze-dried; an artifact, which it is. Especially in the study of the Asian Castro Boy. In the show, actual slides depicting each of the types of Asian Castro Boy were used. For that purpose, I played all the character types in the appropriate attire, props, and stance.

Did I used to be so overwrought? So maudlin? Did I really work off-key monotonous renditions of Nina Simone's "I Want Some Sugar in My Bowl" and Donna Summer's "MacArthur Park," accompanied by tablas no less, into the performance? *What was I thinking?* I ask myself again.

I try to excuse and explain that that was the mode of performance at the time: *...but everyone was doing it!*

"Well, if everyone jumped off a bridge..."

But that's how it goes: as you go along and as you get older, you figure out how to do things better, how to say things better, or more precisely.

You grow into your own language to talk about these things that matter to you.

And if the photo album and its documents survive, they will serve as a gentle reminder of your…, of my meandering journey.

***

Attack of the Man-Eating Lotus Blossoms

Who the Fuck Am I?

(In darkness. Spoken or prerecorded.)
I am Chinese. (I am part of the Chinese diaspora.)/I am gay. (At any point in my life, I always seem to be in love with a man that I'm not sure is in love with me.)/I am a writer. (Once, after a reading, a man came up to me and said, "I didn't understand a word you said, but your reading was very powerful.")/I have an accent./I shave my head./I have tattoos./I am damaged./I am a Joni Mitchell fan./I hate my body./I love my feet./I am a cat owner./I have allergies./I am from what is known as the Third World./I feel invisible./I feel powerless./I feel unattractive./I am bitter./I feel normal./I belong to what they call GENERATION X./I feel alienated./I feel like ASIAN AMERICA'S bastard retard child./I am in pain./I have more closets than I care to imagine./I have bad clothes sense./I like fucking./I like being fucked./I like sucking dick./I like swallowing cum./I like red meat./I am nearsighted./I am uncircumcised./I am vaccinated./I don't know my HIV status anymore./I hate a lot of people./I hate fruit desserts./I like rough sex./I have insomnia./Sometimes, I think I might fall in love with Linda Ronstadt./I want to know for sure./I want to be loved./I hate anyone who loves me./I am drowning./I am the day of openess./I am a plague of locusts./I am crucified./I am bones and paper./I am nothing but dust./I am a work in progress./I am abandoned./I am fucked up./I am totally fucked up./I am a freak./I am between worlds./I am drawing a line in my skull./I am sick./I am recovering./I am in recovery./I am a fucking shit./I am fucking shit out of someone's asshole./I am grim./I am brain-dead./I am a chink./I am a fag./I am ticklish./I am violent when provoked./I am soft-spoken./I am nervous./I am a butterfly./I am a whore./I am a virgin./I am nothing./I am mad./I am a dog./I am repentant./I am baptised./I am saved./I am going to go straight to hell./I am going to visit heaven just to say hello./I am in need of something good./I am the premature ejaculate of a cheap trick./I am short./I should know better./I am a rat./I smell bad./I am not who I want to be./I am regret./I am remorse./I am happy./I am delirious./I am cruel./I am fate./I am poison./I need poison./I need

Justin Chin

oxygen./I need to be abused./I want to scream./I want to cry./I am floating./I am a boring fuck./I am a vegetable./I am a child./I was curious yellow./I am a burden./I am repulsive./I am the splendid parsnips./I am the form of a mouth./I am a dinner of lilies./I am subterranean./I lie like mad./I am in agony./I am spiteful./I am baited with ambition./I am baited with lust./I am naked./I am a black sleeve./I am a cut sleeve./I am the secret life./I am the lines of pleasure./I am mud and honey./I am choking on honey./I am drooling./I am noise./I am not a pipe./I am the last one to be picked./I am broken./I am shame./I am a blade./I am sad./I am empowered./I am not angry anymore./I am numb./I am everything I shouldn't be./I am everything I want to be.

Fagtown

I need a man. I'm running out of time. I know the men in my family, and by the time we hit thirty, we fall apart. Okay, perhaps if we really took care of ourselves, followed all the steps in Lea Salonga's *Health & Beauty for Asian Skin*, perhaps, just perhaps we can make it till thirty-five, but then, it all falls apart: we develop the huge hard round belly, and we all start to smell like my Uncle Jeck Juan—raw pork marinated with beer. It's really quite tragic.

But I live in San Francisco. My friends think that I should have no problems meeting my dream man because they think it's one big huge-ass fag block party. Sort of like it was one huge long concrete *Love Boat* episode. And I live so close to the Castro, too, they tsk at me.

When I first came to San Francisco, I knew I had to find this place called Castro Street. It was February, it was raining, it was cold, I only had a corduroy jacket, I didn't have a map, I just walked and walked and walked. Down Van Ness. Up Market. And amazingly, I ended up on Castro Street. It was as if there was this homing instinct, the same thing that guides salmon to spawn, halibut to the Arctic circle, carrier pigeons with vital information taped to their toes to their destinations. It's really amazing, because I could have just turned off anywhere along the way and I could have ended up in Pacific

Attack of the Man-Eating Lotus Blossoms

Heights or Cow Hollow or Coit Tower or the crookedest Street in the World or (*shudder*) Pier 39. I mean, my first visit to San Francisco would have taken such a different turn. But thanks to my little queer radio signal, that little blip in all our heads that goes FAG/FAG/FAG, that guides us to wherever it is we have to go. (The nonthreatening PC version of that line would read GAY-LESBIAN-BISEXUAL-TRANSGENDERED/GAY-LESBIAN-BISEXUAL-TRANSGENDERED/GAY-LESBIAN-BISEXUAL-TRANSGENDERED; the beat is a little bit off, I know.) But it's true this little blip guided me in my trip to New Orleans. I managed to wander right through the French Quarter right into a fag-bar where a stripper wearing Batman briefs kissed me and I drank way too many $2 Hurricanes and puked all the way back to the Mariott.

But the Castro. The mystical, exciting, exotic, intangible Castro.

Home of butch men with nelly dogs, nelly men with butch bodies.

Home of those annoying little homosexual mustaches.

Yes, the Castro. The alien, intangible, stinking Castro. Literally. I mean with all these fag-dog owners letting their little pooches shit all over the memory of poor little Harvey Milk. And when it rains—whoo—those dried up clumps of dogshit just soak up the water like Body Shop Organic Sponges and they just puff up with their aromatic treasure. And the whole fucking neighborhood smells like the playroom at Gravy Train headquarters.

But to know know know the Castro is to love love love the Castro.

I want to share: I approached my first visit to the Castro like White Folks on their first visit to Chinatown. "Ooooo, how exotic, how bizarre, how thrilling. I wonder if this is a good place to eat. I see a lot of homosexuals are eating here, so it must be an authentic homosexual diner, serving authentic homosexual food."

But as I have known the Castro, let me be your guide to knowing the Castro so you may love the Castro. Using the area's bars as markers and group cluster, the Castro can be

Justin Chin

socio-geographically divided into
1. drunken desperation
2. pathetic desperation
3. desperation in denial
4. upper-middle-class desperation
5. desperation.

How many of the following CASTRO BINGO SQUARES can you collect?

FAGTOWN BINGO

ICE-QUEEN & HER COURT & HANDMAIDENS	TERRIFIED STRAIGHT COUPLE asserting their HETEROSEXUALITY	DIVA without a CAUSE	MR. MULLET	BUTCH with NELLY DOG
BUTCH —but— NELLY	INAPPROPRIATE UNIFORM QUEEN	FAG from STONEHENGE	LEATHER TITLE HOLDER WEARING SASH while GROCERY SHOPPING	SPEED QUEEN
HOLIER-than-THOU BIKE FAG	Fag of 1,000,000 flyers	★	CLONE-A-RAMA	total clueless fag
EVIL VEGAN FAG	HE WHO HOMOSEXUALITY IS WASTED ON	SUPER ANGRY FAG	5'1" thinks 'DON'T PANIC' T-shirts r' FUNNY	DAIRY QUEEN
FREEDOM -RINGS-	2 (or more) fags arguing outside a bar (extra pt if either uses Paula Abdul song lyrics: "But my love is for Real!" You're a cold-hearted snake!")	ULTRA HIGH MAINTENANCE FAG — gimme attention! NOW	FAG WHO REMEMBERS that you accidentally smiled at him once 7 YEARS AGO in a bar that no longer exists	TRYING to be BEAR but not quite in the woods

52

Attack of the Man-Eating Lotus Blossoms

There is this bar in the Castro called Headquarters. It's a uniform bar. It's a fetish thing, you know, uniforms—army, navy, police, United Airlines, McDonald's, KFC. Way kinky stuff, out of my league.

So here's this Uniform Bar and all these big facial-haired buffed-out men looking butch are spilling out of the doors like the tequila in a margarita on the *USS Poseidon*, and out of the door, along with the smell of sweaty Castro queens in uniforms and rank beer, comes some thumping music. What do they play in a uniform bar, I wonder? I lean in. It can't be! It is. No. Yes. It's RuPaul's "Supermodel": "*Turn to the Left/Now Turn to the Right/Sashay/Chanté/Sashay/Chanté...*"

And suddenly I get the mental image of Gen. Colin Powell sashaying and chanté-ing on the dance floor while Gen. Norman Schwarzkopf on his 8th Chocolate Chu-Chu for the evening (because I'd like to believe that he can't handle anything stronger than a Chocolate Chu-Chu) by the cigarette machine, cruises him and they plan surgical strikes on how to invade each other's body orifices in the restroom. And then I realize that that mental picture sums up all I or anyone really needs to know about the Castro.

With any Fag City, it is important to know the Art of Scamming. To Scam. To look at passersby in a subtle, tilting, discreet yet firmly flirtatious manner that says, FUCK ME, DAMMIT!
So let me present:

Zen and the Art of Cruising at Cafe Hairdo.

1. The Deer Reaches for the Berries.
(From seated position, the performer arches back full while lifting his head as if deer were reaching for berries.)

2. The Horse Looks Under the Shrub.
(From seated position, the performer swoops down gracefully as if horse were looking under shrub.)

3. The Lizard on the Rock Watches the World Go By.
(From seated position, the performer moves head slowly 180 degrees to and fro as if a lizard were on a hot rock watching the world go by.)

Justin Chin

4. The Ostrich Is Startled by a Sound.
(From seated position, the performer snaps head 180 degrees to and fro, up, down, and askance in a jitter as if an ostrich were startled by a sound.)

5. The Horny Homosexual Touches Himself.
(From any position, the performer touches himself in the nether regions as if he were dancing for dimes in some seedy gay dive outside of Fresno.)

But strange as it may seem, that ugly, glittering three block radius has a strange hold over me.

And everytime I hear an ambulance screaming along the street, plunging its flashing red lights and wailing screams into the Castro, I start to wonder if it's making a beeline to someone's home to take someone's lover away, to remove a body that once desired with a queer breath as this body desires with its own queer breath.

I wonder if that ambulance scream is the stand-in dubbed voices of those left behind who are too lost, too sad, too weary to scream anymore. I wonder if that scream is like a wonderful foreign film that has been dubbed into familiar language, a safe language, where mood, music, scenes, and scenery flicker and flicker and flicker endlessly flicker in a mere language barely potent enough to carry the weight of grief.

I wonder if those flashing red lights are the physical shape of that little click in your head, that switch that kicks in when you least expect it and controls your rage, bitterness, and sadness like a Panama Canal of your grief.

I wonder if those red flashing lights are the grim retro-disco urgent reminder for the next generation of how we live now.

And standing in the red flash, and standing in the blanket of sirens, suddenly, I pretend to understand why RuPaul's "Supermodel" blasting out of a uniform-leather bar all makes sense.

I pretend to know why a 6'5" black drag queen's ode to multimillion-dollar ultraglamourous supermodels should be blasting out of a leather-uniform bar in the Castro.

Attack of the Man-Eating Lotus Blossoms

And suddenly, the Castro doesn't smell like wet dog shit. The desperation peters out into some playful adolescent yearning. The men with mustaches and dogs seem quaint and picturesque.

And suddenly, the mental image of Powell and Schwarzkopf is replaced by that of two men, two people, two bodies who need everything in their cupboards, everything in their closets, everything in their lives to help them make it to the next day, the next bed, the next lover, the next good time, the next safe time.

And even as I hate the Castro, I still need to go into it from time to time, because it gives me something I need, some aching need that pulls everything I am into a tight little ball and releases it just right, just as I know what my man can do for me. It's like how gravity works to hold us on the ground and let's us walk, let's us run.

And I know we need everything we can afford. We need every promise, every remnant, every hope, every scrap to keep our queer desires breathing.

So, baby: Use fantasy, use fetish, use Jesus, use Marx, use desire, use reality, use gloom, use joy, use bravado, use guns, use vision, use language, use madness, use yr horses, use yr time, use gods, use angels, use pills, use a desert, use a wash, use insecticide, use the mental, use the framer, use flight, use pilgrimage, use a flesh, use a fracture, use darkness, use damage, use sweetness, use toxin, use beauty, use them all, baby.

97·CHINK, or, Baby, How Do I Look Tonight?

(During "How Do I Look?" the performer pulls a folded piece of paper out of his pocket. He tears bits and chunks off, tossing them on the floor, then carefully unfolding the paper, reveals it to be a chain of paper dolls. Then, plucking off one doll at a time, he slowly eats each doll until the end of the section.)

Justin Chin

I. How Do I Look?
1. Rule #1: Everyone is white unless stated otherwise.

> Example: Joe, Sam, an African American, and their Asian American friend Stanley went on a picnic at the beach where they met Thereza, a Latina, and her friend Jane.

Hence,
> Sample Question #1: Who is white?
> Model Answer #1: Joe, Jane, and apparently, someone named Ronald.

> Sample Question #2: If the five characters are arrested at the beach for indecent exposure, whose ethnicity will be named in the local newspaper?
> Model Answer #2: Sam, Stanley, and Thereza.

> Sample Question #3: If a news photographer shows up and takes pictures of the picnic, who will be prominently featured in the gay news weekly and who will be the only one named in the caption?
> Model Answer #3: Joe (but only if he's really buffed) or Joe and whoever he's hugging at the time (but only if both are really cute).

2. Like all male bodies in gay culture, everything is predicated on the image and concepts of the beautiful body. If the average gay man is to stroll through the racks of titillating images, he will see a vast buffet of white bodies, and at the end of the buffet table are the "splashes of color that make any buffet table entertaining."

The gay Asian male body, however, is a different creature, and certain rules apply to it. For the uninitiated, who are eager to learn and experience more, here are some things that you must know about the the gay Asian body that will help you in your research as you peruse the racks at your local bookstore or library:

Attack of the Man-Eating Lotus Blossoms

1. The desired image is buffed and muscular or slim and lean.

(Attach a picture of a mung bean here.)

2. Body hair and/or fat is utterly undesirable.

(Attach a picture of silken tofu here.)

3. Severe ectomorphism becomes a fetishistic quality.

(Attach a picture of a starving goat here.)

4. Nipples are not important and are never emphasized.

(Attach a picture of third superfluous nipple here.)

5. The background and the objects surrounding the body are almost as important as the body.
    Suggested backgrounds and objects are: i) Oriental vases and urns; ii) masks and costumes representing ancient dynastic histories; iii) silk; iv) bamboo, pussy willows, and the most

potent object of all, chrysanthemums.

(Attach two close-up details from Oriental rugs here, or fiber samples from Oriental rugs.)

(True testimony:)
"Hello. My name is Peter Wong. And (*squeak*). Hello? Hello? Yes. My name is Peter Wong and I am a real person, not a paid model. Like most Chinese men, I used to be very frigid and uptight in bed but ever since I started surrounding my pillows with chrysanthemums...

Ever since I've surrounded my bed with chrysanthemums, man, I've been fucking and sucking like the horniest cow this side of the YangHo River. My repertoire of sex acts has expanded and the other day, while cooking for my boyfriend, I used this bottle of Mazola Corn Oil, six pounds of cooked Spam, and..."

3. Primary Sources
The Nob Hill Cinema's Asian Week runs an advertisement in the local gay newsweekly. Year after year, the strip joint features a week of Asian male performers. Year after year, they do not ever use a real photograph to advertise the week, only drawings of buffed Asian men with headbands inscribed with some Oriental language. (For headbands, see *The Karate Kid Parts 1 through 3*.) When a real photo was finally used, it was of a group of Asian male dragon boat racers ripped from a travel catalog. The photo, reduced to a small strip, hides behind Chip Daniels' and Señor Latino's hips, the other main attraction.

The promotional image that most sticks in my mind is one from two years ago. Asian Week featured a drawing of a buffed Japanese man in a headband and jockstrap, tied in Oriental Rope Harness fashion. He is gagged. His legs are bound and his hands are tied behind his back. His eyes are simultaneously vacant and intense. There is a tube of lube

Attack of the Man-Eating Lotus Blossoms

beside him and a huge black dildo lying on the floor, pointing at his perineum.

> Sample Question #1: Who is using the dildo on the cartoon Japanese man?
>
> Sample Question #2: Does the cartoon Japanese man enjoy it?
>
> Sample Question #3: Can the cartoon Japanese man protest if he doesn't enjoy it?
>
> Sample Question #4: Will the cartoon Japanese man protest if he doesn't enjoy it?
>
> Sample Question #5: Is this just a cartoon?

II. How Do I Sound?
"Hello. This is 97-CHINK. If you want to play, you must press your Visa or Mastercard number. Now. If you want a submissive Oriental houseboy to do your laundry, then suck your dick, press 1 now. If you want a Thai go-go boy to touch his body onstage just for you, press 2 now. If you want a hot hung Filipino youth to worship your body, press 3 now. If you want an alternative menu, press 4 now. For voice mail, press 5 now.

(xxx-xxx-xxxx-xxxx). #. beep. 2. #.

"Hello. My name is Huang. I just come in from working in the padi field and boy, I tell you, am I sweaty, I must take a bath. I like taking showers because it make me feel so clean. Here, I leave the door open so you can talk to me while I shower okay. Ooo. The water feels so good on my skin. I got very good skin, very soft even though I work in the sun and get real good tan. Do you like to feel my skin? That's okay, I don't mind you feeling my skin. It's so soft, yah? Oh, I'm so silly, I forgot to bring the soap with me. Can you please get it for me? Thank you, you are so kind. Oh. I can't reach my back. Please, can you please help me? Oh yes, you are too kind. I must get super clean, please scrub harder. Oh yes. Thank you. Please, don't soap close to my private parts otherwise I get hard and then I get very shy. Oh dear, my cock is now getting hard from all that soap water. Oh no, if I go out now, my father will see my cock standing and he will get angry, what should I do. What? Okay, but please, gently okay? I'm very scared doing this. If you use your mouth, it will be gentler than your hand? Okay. But please be careful. I don't ever do this before...

(beep) (#)

"Hello. My name is Aurelio Eduardo Concepcíon Batongbacal. But you can call me Eddy because you are my friend. I like watching movies, reading stories, watching TV, and making new friends like you. I like to have friends all over the world so I can visit them and they can visit me when they come to Manila and I can show them all the beautiful sights of the city and show them just how beautiful the Filipino culture is. The people are also so friendly. But sometimes I get so lonely because I don't have many gay friends, that's why I'm so happy that you're my friend. I like you because you are so manly. Can I ask you a personal question? Sorry. I shy to ask you. But do you have chest hair? Oh, I like that very much. Can I please feel it? Oh yes, did anyone tell you you look like Magnum? Yes, you do. I think Magnum is very handsome. I think you are very handsome. Is it true that Americans have big, you know. Can I see? OOOO! It's so big. I'm so scared! What? It's not painful? But it's so big! Slowly and easy? Please, you teach me, please? I want to learn how to play with big American cocks, because they are more fun! So you teach Eddy, okay?

III. *Do You Know Me?*
Hello. My name is Peter Lum. Do you recognize me? I'm an actor. Perhaps not. Let's try again.

"Hey, do you come to the steam baths often?" Recognize me now? That was the line I used in *Steam Boat Dragons* before I fucked Lance Michaels in the ass.

No? Perhaps you know me by my other name, my stage names: Kimo. Thu Minh. Kwan. Jeong Chew. Chris Fujimoto. Perhaps you know me by my reputation. I'm the only working gay Asian male porn star in America who's a top. You might have

Attack of the Man-Eating Lotus Blossoms

seen me in films like *Platoon Dragon*, *Shanghai Dragons*, *Dragon Mission*, *Dragon Meat*, *Dragons*, *Dragons 2: China Heat*, and *Enter the Dragon's Ass*.

Yes. In my first film, *Red Dragon Heat*, the director said for Scott Folberg to fuck me in the ass in a scene at the school gym, but then, Scott was on something and he couldn't get his dick hard so I improvised, and I fucked him in the ass. The scene was hot. And I discovered that I actually can fuck white boys in the ass—and enjoy it too! Wow, what a revelation.

In my last film, *Hard Dragon*, I got to fuck six white boys because I'm the star now. I even get creative input on the shoots and the scene. Like this one scene where I meet Larion Lasley at the doctor's office, I'm supposed to play the janitor while he plays the patient. But I tell the director, "I want to be a doctor!" And so I played a doctor. I don't want to perpetuate stereotypes that Asians are coolies and low-class workers. And in another scene, the director wants me to come in a samurai outfit! But then I tell him, *The character is Chinese!!! How can you use a samurai outfit?* So we rewrote the scene. I wore a kung fu outfit instead! These things are important, you know.

But my favorite film is *Penetrate the Dragon*. In this one, I get to fuck this other Asian guy. It was a difficult scene. And I had to prepare myself for days to do it. Later, I found out that the guy I was fucking, Wilson Woo, also had similar fears and had to prepare for days by looking at Latino porn magazines and masturbating to them, just like what I did. We did not use Asian porn because it's so funny you just cannnot jack, or it makes us really uncomfortable. The scene that Wilson and I did was in the backroom of a Chinese restaurant. He and I are there with our white dates but then we pretend to go to the bathroom while actually we fuck! Great, huh? Then later, our dates discover us and we all fuck! This is a ground-breaking porn film for gay Asians, I think.

Anyhow, I don't think I'm going to be in the porn business for long. Too demanding. I mean, I'm lucky that I got a nice big dick that photographs well, but I think I still want to go to college. I want to major in Asian American Studies and Theater, you know. Or Philosophy and then get an MBA. One day, I also want to make a feature-length film about Asian Americans. In fact, I already have a film script that I'm shopping around. It's about 200 pages long with good dialogue, lots of double entendres and symbolism.

IV. But How Do I Really Look?
THE ASIAN CASTRO BOY: A STUDY

Kingdom:	Animalia
Phylum:	Chordate
Class:	Mammalia
Order:	Omnivora
Family:	Hominidae
Genus:	*Homo sapiens*
Species:	*Orientali Castronitus*

Habitat: Castro Street, San Francisco, United States of America.

The *Orientali Castronitus* is primarily found roaming Castro Street between Market and 19th Streets. Occasionally a few may stray to the smaller side streets. They number in the dozens and are best found all day on Saturday and Sunday, though many are spotted in the evenings too.

Distinguishing Features of Various Subspecies of *Orientali Castronitus*:
1. Orientali Castronitus Fluffinitus
  Features: Girbaud. Klein. Ralph Lauren or any outfit bought at trendy overpriced store in a not-so-good, but still moderately safe, neighborhood. Good shoes. BodyGlove, Spandex, Lycra, bicycle shorts (even though they cab everywhere). Tight little denim shorts.
  Hair: Well groomed. Moussed—very flammable. Gelled and sculptured into a hard shell to protect against elements and worthy of being placed in the middle of a ten-course Chinese dinner. May be hidden under specially selected cap on a bad hair day.

Attack of the Man-Eating Lotus Blossoms

(Using pastels, sketch picture of
Orientali Castronitus Fluffinitus *here.)*

Group Site: The Midnight Sun with three pieces of picture ID ready.
Diet: Nouvelle Cuisine. Thai restaurants. Bran muffin and Diet Coke at Village Deli.
Distingushing Call: "Discriminating against people of color? What? I don't know. I'm really not political. I just want to dance and have fun and meet someone cute, okay?"

2. *Orientali Castronitus Withhaolius*
Features: Stuck to his white companion. Either on arm, on hip, or with invisible leash. Eyes averted from any other white men, but will stare straight into other Asians' eyes, then quickly look away.
Hair: See *Orientali Castronitus Fluffinitus*, or whatever his companion wants.

(Using water colors, sketch picture of
Orientali Castronitus Withhaolius *here.)*

Group Site: Wherever his companion wants.
Diet: Thai restaurants, Chinese restaurants, Castro Hibachi (for the ambience and presumably authentic food, the kind that you can eat lots of and still don't gain weight).
Distinguishing Call: "I can't talk to you, my boyfriend is here." "Please don't touch me, I have a boyfriend."

Justin Chin

3. *Orientali Castronitus Activistus*
   Features: ACT UP T-shirt or Queer Nation/United Colors T-shirt (ripped-off sleeves optional). Jeans (rips optional). Necklace-thing hanging from neck. Glasses from chic urban desinger. Clean polished Doc Martens. In hand or backpack, either i) *The Collected Works of Michel Foucault*; ii) *Collected Poems of Audre Lourde*; iii) *Woman, Native, Other* by Trinh T. Minh-Ha; iv) *Queer in America* by Michelangelo Signorile; or v) *Mandala Symbolism* by C.G. Jung.
   Hair: Functional. Flat-top.

   (Using blood from the Imperialists' hands, sketch picture of Orientali Castronitus Activistus *here.)*

   Group Site: A Different Light Bookstore. Flyering table at Castro and 18th. Hot n' Hunky. Escape from New York Pizza or Marcello's Pizza. Castro Theater.
   Diet: Diner food. 24-hour-joint food. Pizza slices.
   Distinguishing Call: "Act Up! Fight Back!" "We're Queer! We're Here!" "Die, Gay White Man!" "Asian Power." "Empowerment."

4. *Orientali Castronitus Alternativus*
   Features: Black clothes. Bags under eyes. Sneer/growl. Plaid shirts, scruffy Doc Martens or any boots, ripped jeans or cutoff trousers. Knife, tattoos, and piercings optional. Alienated aura.
   Hair: Buzz cut, shaved, stubble, or none.

Attack of the Man-Eating Lotus Blossoms

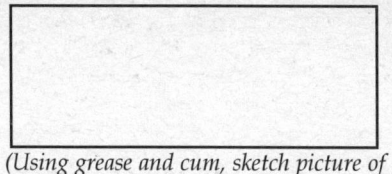

(Using grease and cum, sketch picture of
Orientali Castronitus Alternativus *here.)*

Group Site: Usually not found in Castro. But may be seen at A Different Light Bookstore or Escape from New York Pizza or sometimes at Castro Theater.
Diet: Cheap food. Coffee. Alcohol optional.
Distinguishing Call: "Fuck off." "Whaddya want?" "Die Fluffy Scum."

Approaching the *Orientali Castronitus*
While myth and years of conventional wisdom have it that the *Orientali Castronitus* are friendly creatures and may be approached at any time without repercussions, this has in modern years been proven to be a fallacy.

Some subspecies of the *Orientali Castronitus,* such as the *Fluffinitus,* may be approached with ease, but the others may not be. For instance, the *Withhaolius* have been known to snap back or run like a startled fawn when approached. In some eyewitness accounts, the haole with the *Withhaolius* displayed severely violent territorial behavior.

The two most unapproachable are the *Activistus* and the *Alternativus*. The *Activistus* may start yelling at you; and the *Alternativus* may stab you in the gut. Be warned!

Now that you are familiar with the species *Orientali Castronitus*, feel free to roam the Castro without fear or trepidation. If you still wish to learn more about them, you should ask the reference librarian at your local library for books about them, though very little has been written on the subject.

For the adventurous ones who still might want to actually approach one of the *Orientali Castronitus*, here are some suggested opening lines:

Justin Chin

For the *Fluffinitus*:
1. "Where are you from?"
2. "Where's a good club/restaurant/place to buy shirts around here?"

For the *Withhaolius*:
1. "You're so lucky to have such a good-looking companion." (Note: Always address the companion and not the *Orientali Castronitus*.)

For the *Activistus*:
1. "What do you think of (insert name of congressional bill here)?"
2. "I don't understand the issues in this flyer, can you please explain it to me?"

For the *Alternativus*:
1. "How can anyone buy the Sex Pistols on CD, man? That's so stupid! How can you understand its meaning then?"
2. "Who does your tattz, man?"
(Note: Though it may seem harmless, *NEVER* say: "I like your tattoos, what are they actually? They must mean something, have some symbolism. Tell me!")

V. Do You Love Me?
(Real letter. I no kid you.)
An Open Letter to Justin Chin:

My reaction to your awful whining writing, Justin? Well, I reacted on several different levels. I was immediately struck by the anger, the hatred, the rage, the venom that poured forth from your pen and I thought to myself, "This guy has really been hurt. He's in a lot of pain." And thinking this, my eyes got moist, as indeed they are as I write this. I've never been into S&M. I don't enjoy pain, either my own or someone else's. And when I imagine the pain that you had to go through in order to be filled up with so much rage, my heart goes out to you.

Justin, you seem to rage at everyone: you're angry at us whites who are prejudiced against Asians; you're angry at those of us who are attracted to Asians and even Asian culture, ridiculing even our mismatched collections of Asian art, our

Attack of the Man-Eating Lotus Blossoms

attempts to use chopsticks and to learn other cultural customs. You are even angry at other Asians who are attracted to whites. I wonder, do you ever wear blue jeans or use a fork?

Justin, none of us likes to be nothing more than a sex object. More than once an Asian has been disappointed in me because I *didn't* have hair on my chest. And, on the flip side of that, I have experienced many times the silly gushing of an Asian over my blue eyes. But, Justin, in all of these cases, we went beyond that initial reaction and developed relationships (not just sexual ones, either) that were based on more than my blue eyes or their silky smooth hairless skin.

We are all humans, Justin, and how can we explain what it is that makes our crotches tingle? Can you honestly say to us that your own physical attractions to others have been totally without objectification? Have you never experienced fetish-like qualities in your own sexual urges?

Your anger is destroying you, Justin. It is poison that is eating you alive. And that's such a waste. Yes, Justin, there is injustice in this world. There is racism, discord, prejudice, discrimination, evil, pollution, hunger, poverty, and all kinds of wretchedness. And we should all work to change this.

And we can do this, motivated by love and compassion. Like Mother Teressa (sic).

Or with anger and rage. Like you.

And one more thing, Justin. My name is "D——." What does my name mean, you ask?

It means "Beloved."

D—— S——, Psychologist
Dallas, Texas

An Invocation for Mr. S—— and People Like Him in the Hopes That Their Moist Eyes Would Blind Them So They Stumble Off The Pavement Into the Path of a Beer Truck.
Dear Mr. S——:

Thank you for giving me your bleeding heart. I promptly took it to the organ bank. They were quite pleased. I got 76¢ for it. It wasn't enough for bus fare. I walked home. When I got home, there was a message on the answering machine. It was the organ bank. They couldn't use the heart after all—it had bled itself blue. I could keep the 76¢ though, they said. So I'm sending you back your heart postage paid. Enclosed are a couple of tissues for you to wipe your eyes too. We wouldn't want your tears to blind you lest you fall off the pavement and get crushed by a truck loaded with Miller Drafts.

Because I was so excited when I received your heart, I rushed straight to the organ bank instead of writing a thank-you note immediately. Where are my manners! So I am writing now to thank you for your heart and tears and to respond to your kind kind note.

I'm feeling much better now. I have been able to feel so much more centered and calm ever since you explained to me that the roots of my oppression, the pain and the anger that I was feeling, were something that I consciously chose to enjoy, like anchovies on an extra-cheese, deep-crust pizza, boxer shorts, armpit sniffing, and sadomasochism.

Also, I'm glad you so understand the racism and the marginalization that I've experienced and am able to advise me on how to deal with all these oppressions. Honestly, without you, I'm nothing! I did notice all that sexual imagery in your note—all those spurting pens, etc. Why, Mr. S——, if I didn't know better, I'd think you were being quite naughty indeed!

Oh yes. How I wish I was more like Mother Teresa. Then I too could be worshipped and adored as a wrinkled colonialist. She's the last of a pure breed, you know. I'm sure there's nothing I like to do better than rescue poor sick folks and make sure they know their class and place in this world, all so they can get their true reward in the glorious golden realms of heaven. (But Bless Me Father for I Have Sinned.)

Don't tell anyone this, but since you asked, I've always wanted to be an ice-pick-wielding fag given to stabbing the poor hapless sap I just fucked. Oh dear, I wish I could just be satisfied with frottage, heavy kissing, and foot-licking.

Oh dear me, I have to run now. Got to fire up the Norelco Wet/Dry Shaver™ so I can keep my silky smooth hairless skin up to par. Once again, thanks so much for your kind love and compassion.

Hugs and kisses,
Justin Chin
San Francisco, California

Attack of the Man-Eating Lotus Blossoms

P.S. I'll just simply die of hunger without my lacquered chopsticks! And I'm rarely seen without my slit-up-to-my-hips cheong-sam!

VI. Epilogue

When I was little my whole family said I looked like a seal. Growing up, the image of beauty and attractiveness was always the other: the Japanese, the Korean, and especially, the Eurasian. And in my family, my brother was the good-looking one. When there was a family gathering, there would always be some remark that my brother was so damn good-looking (and his good grades and footballing skills probably helped in their estimation). Then the gaze would turn to me and they would ask me what I was going to do with my life.

The funny thing about all this is that the last time I went home, my family said that I was beginning to look Japanese. As if that wasn't bad enough, store owners also thought I was Japanese, and greetings of *Konichiwa* followed me as an inticement to enter their store. And when I did and when they found out that I was merely local, they refused to sell me an under-the-counter cheap knock-off imitation Titoni watch.

Perhaps I'm being terribly shallow, whining on and on about beauty and attractiveness. Why do we care so much about beauty and image? Why do children's stories and fairy tales tell us that good people are beautiful and bad people ugly?

But more than that, researchers have found that attractive people tend to get further in life. They found that attractive people do better in school, work, and relationships.

In one experiment, researchers attached to an eight-year-old child's dismal school and test records an attractive photo of a child and to the same copy of the report, an unattractive photo of a child. Nearly twice as many of the teachers who reviewed the file recommended that the unattractive child be sent to a special-education class.

In another experiment, a mediocre college-level sophomore essay (about some inane topic like WHY I LIKE SUMMER) was sent to teams of graders. To the very same essay, the researchers attached photos of the supposed writer, again attractive and unattractive people. The essay with the

attractive photo attached consistently received higher marks.
No shit.
Researchers have found that people who think themselves unattractive are more prone to mental illness later in life.

In a study of 17,000 professional men, researchers found that those over six feet received a higher salary and were promoted faster.

And it's really not different in our little homo-heavens, our little gay ghettos. Perhaps it's even worse. Perhaps it's even more worse when you're colored. Because the First Law of Homoculture states: everyone is white, healthy, well-groomed, has pectoral muscles, is straight-acting, and is "just like everyone else" unless stated otherwise. And the Second Law of Homoculture states: the bodies of those stated otherwise are "types," definable objects bound by measurable boundaries, bodies that remain at rest until a force nudges them into a constant adoration.

It's pretty telling that the one of the only four references to Asians in *The New Joy of Gay Sex* (1992), that instruction manual for the homosexual lifestyle, that wonderful tome of homo-wisdom that no genetically born fag should be without, should come under the heading NEW MACHO IMAGE. We're told by the authors that the ACT UP look suits all racial types, as if that's going to help us. The other three references are found in the sections RACISM, TYPES (where we learn that the slender Asian may not always want to play the shy geisha all the time and that one should make allowances for this), and SEX WITH ANIMALS (where we learn that the Chinese are known to have "love affairs" with geese).

The First Law of Homoculture.
The Second Law of Homoculture.

"Nobody ever called me beautiful and meant it.
"Nobody ever called me beautiful while they were sober.
"Nobody ever called me beautiful out of bed.
"Nobody ever called me beautiful without his dick somewhere in me.
"Nobody ever called me beautiful because I'm probably not."

Attack of the Man-Eating Lotus Blossoms

The First Law of Homoculture.
The Second Law of Homoculture.

What do you see?

Damage

There are three parts to an insect's body: the head, the thorax, and the abdomen. According to a science book that I read years ago, the insect will die immediately if its abdomen is crushed; not so for the head or the thorax. Something about the spiracles, the breathing apparatus of the insect.

I'm having a roach infestation. The rains and the heavy construction next door (they're building a new lot of apartments) have driven the little roaches into my flat. My roommate has sprinkled boric acid in all the dark crevices following the instructions in her book of natural home remedies. Just to be on the safe side, she also bought fifty little roach traps and placed them strategically beside the boric acid. One way or the other, she was sure the roaches would die, and this way, they could choose their method of death.

I chanced upon a roach the other day, right beside the Mr. Coffee while I was trying to brew an eight-cup pot of Sumatra Dark. Thinking it a safe bet to squish the bug instead of waiting for it to commit suicide in the Boric Acid/Dow Roach Trap Final Exit test, I did the deed with the box of unbleached Melitta cone coffee filters.

Interestingly, the tip of the box hit the poor roach squarely on its abdomen. But as cruel fate would have it, the roach did not die. The force of the box on the roach's abdomen only caused that unfortunate insect's intestines to shoot out of its ass. It's all kind of like squeezing some Silly String out of a tube at an office party. But an even crueler fate was that the poor traumatized roach couldn't run away, crawl into a dark corner, and lick its wounds, as the viscosity of its wet entrails on the acetate countertop caused the roach to be almost glued to the spot. The burden of dragging one's entrails. In human terms, it would be like sloshing in wet boots in knee-high mud, or if your wedding-gown train were soaking wet and pinning you down, unable to make it to the altar.

Justin Chin

To make a long story short, I finished the deed with my roommate's coffee mug.

Later, I told a friend about this rather queer episode. "By all means, the poor roach should have died, but it didn't," I said. My friend pointed out that it would be the opposite in chickens. It's a well known fact that when chickens' heads are hacked off, they are still able to run about headless for at least five minutes before collapsing into a bloody mess. Workers at chicken farms have testified to this. Humans, on the other hand, would die if a dime tossed off the middle of the Empire State Building hit them squarely on the head.

Technically, you could lop off an insect's head and it could still live. The only thing is that it wouldn't have a brain or a method to eat. But everything else—heart, breathing, legs—would still function.

The whole premise would make a great horror flick: ten-foot-long headless insects invade small town. The only glitch would be that as hideous as they would look, the monster insects wouldn't be able to bite or eat anyone.

Understand the importance of blood.

When I was seventeen, I tried to commit suicide twice. The first time, I swallowed a handful of antihistamines. It didn't produce the desired effect and I only woke with incredibly dry nostrils. The second time, I swallowed a handful of blood pressure pills. Again, it didn't produce the desired effect, which was to let my blood flow slow down until it became a trickle and then the entire circulation calmed down like the Dead Sea. But that didn't happen and I only woke the next afternoon with a strange buzz, a massive headache, a terrible nausea, and a fucking depressed bitchy attitude about it all. Of course like most suicide attempts, failed or successful, I thought a lot about the means of the act. I thought a lot about more drastic means like:

Jumping off a building. Hanging. Slashing wrists. So dramatic. So Hong Kong melodrama.

But I felt that these were either too painful or way too messy. It's hell trying to commit suicide while not being able to put aside that Virgo compulsiveness. So I decided that blood

Attack of the Man-Eating Lotus Blossoms

was the best way to do it. But unfortunately, or fortunately, I cheated blood.

You may cheat blood but you can't cheat its flow.

I have a recurrent dream about this. In this dream, I'm sitting in the kitchen. I'm looking for the veins in my left arm. I'm holding a knife and slowly using the tip to nip into my skin, the little bit of flesh, and eventually flicking the membrane of the vein open, all with a delicacy reserved for dissection and cakemaking. I'm sitting on the kitchen floor with the top of my vein in my left arm, the skinnier arm, open as if the vein were a water hose and I merely peeled the top off to look into the tube. I watch my blood flowing down my arm and, under that vein, the blood flow up the arm. In reality, blood in your arteries flows as fast as a midnight bus on an open road, but in my dream, the flow merely trickles, a garden hose in the middle of a drought. Then someone, different people each time, enters the kitchen and I will wake—thrown back into the slow-motion roller-coaster ride that is my life.

When you die, you may become either one of three things: angels; ghosts; demons.

Consider the options:
Angels get to gently whisk around and inspire people to do good things and beautiful things. Ghosts get to strike a pose and look winsome—strictly for the poseurs. Demons get to dart about and possess the living.

When I die, I want to come back as a demon and possess all those attitudinal shits in all those clubs and bars that have wronged me and make them have horrible breakouts, bad hair, potbellies, the pox (maybe syphillis if I really feel like working it), and best of all, a proclivity for bad fashion decisions.

When I die, I want to come back as a demon and possess various people in my life who judged me wrong. I want to drag them out to some cheap motel with the scuzziest trick, get them on their knees and to beg to lick cum/spit/shit off the floor. I want to make them want to take it in their ass while citing prophetic scriptures. I want to leave their body the very precise moment they feel that regret of hot jism squirt up their rectum.

Think of all the ramifications of being able to possess bodies. Anyone from politicians or lawmakers to your neighbors and friends. Think of all the sheer fun. Think of all the people you could fuck over and nothing would be able to save you.

But for the living,
somewhere, something is always waiting to save you

Somewhere, Jesus will crawl down from his cross, discard his loin cloth at yr feet and kiss you until it's all better

Somewhere, Buddha's bones will flavor yr tea

Somewhere, yr therapist wants to finger-fuck you

Somewhere, Louise Hay and Marianne Williamson will get out of their limousines, sneak into yr bed and whisper sweet affirmations into yr skull until you go blind

Somewhere, the Virgin Mary is making you lick her pits

Somewhere, the Prophet is watching her

& somewhere, the suicide man is never sad

& somewhere. & somewhere.

My mother tells me that I was born a Christian.
My father tells me that I was born with potential.
My grandmother tells me that I was born with little fuss.
The queer community tells me that I was born gay.
The United Nations tells me that I was born in the Third World.
    (Got the vaccination scars to prove it.)
Politicians tell me that I was born at the most opportune time
    in the nation's history.
Scientists tell me that I was born with a bit of my brain bigger
    than 85 percent of the population.
The church tells me that I was born a sinner.

Attack of the Man-Eating Lotus Blossoms

Psychologists tell me that I was born to learn.
Science tells me that I was born.
All this is supposed to make me feel mighty real.

I was going out with this man
& he said to me,

HE SAID "why do you have to do that to your body"

& I SAID "do what"
& HE SAID "you know"

& I SAID "no, what"
& HE SAID "why do you have to sleep with all those other men"

& I SAID "well, not much I can do about that now is there"
& HE SAID "you're exactly my type but why do you have to do that to your body"

"I wish you were really shy and bookish, you'd spend all day in the library and you'd have big balls with big loads of cum to shoot in my mouth" HE SAID
"well, except for the big balls and big load of cum, I can pretend, but that wouldn't be the same, would it" I SAID
"no, no, that's okay, just pretend" HE SAID

People always want to know.
When was the first time I had sex with a man.
When was the first time I had sex with a man and liked it.
When was the first time I took some cock in my mouth.
When was the first time I was in love.
When was the first time I knew I liked dick.
When was the first time I saw my father naked.
When was the first time I saw my mother naked.
When was the first time I noticed hair growing on my dick.
When was the first time I got my balls licked in a toilet.
When was the first time I swallowed.
When was the first time I had a good load of cum dripping out of my ass.

Justin Chin

Nobody ever wants to know when was the last time I had a good load of cum dripping out of my ass.

The first time I ever had sex was at the age of thirteen just before shop in the first-floor toilet of Swiss Cottage Secondary School. This man sat behind me on the bus to school and put his foot in the crack of the seat. It was an old bus and the seats were two cushions: seat and backrest, both in a metal frame; there was a split between the two and he pressed the tip of his shoe against me.

I glanced behind and caught his reflection in the window as the bus shuttled along a row of trees that would darken the window enough to allow me to catch a glimpse of him: ugly, skimpy mustache, looked like the kind of man you'd see at shopping malls hanging out with nothing to do, the sort I'd walk across the street to avoid because he looked like the "short, tight-fitting polo shirt, polyester slacks, slim gold jewelry" type that would stab you with a bearing scraper if you looked at him wrong.

He followed me when I transferred buses and sat beside me. He apologized for touching my rear. I ignored him. After a fidgety silence, he suddenly but nervously placed his hand on my crotch and frantically asked, pleaded, panicked for me to cover that touch with my school bag, and the Adidas canvas shielded some pervert's embarrassed thrill from the rest of the passengers.

Now when people ask, I remember it as different: he was the most gorgeous hunk, he worked in a bank, he smelled good, and we came together after he sucked me. I did not gag on his dick. I did not nearly vomit up my breakfast from the smell of his dick. I did not try to run out only to be grabbed from behind, slapped across the face. He did not force his dick into my mouth while leaning over to whisper in my ear how I would get expelled if I was caught. I was not late for class because I shitted on myself after he tried to stick his dick into my ass without telling me. I did not spend a half hour crying in a toilet stall, cleaning myself up while praying to the Almighty Lord God Jesus Christ for forgiveness. All that did not happen: we just sucked a little, he kissed me on the mouth but I did not like it, and we watched each other come.

Attack of the Man-Eating Lotus Blossoms

Only I can fuck with my memories:
And all those pity fucks. (Did not happen!)
All those boring fucks. (Are suddenly great!)
All that rough sex when I didn't want it. (Was so tender you could cry!)
That incident in the restroom of the mall that made me bleed up the ass for three days. (Was the hottest sex ever! And he called!)

Only I can fuck with my memories and I can't stop there:
H. who was beaten to near death for looking too damn good in a dress. (Snapped his way out of there with so much shade, you could have put on a shadow play!)
And J. who killed himself. (Was hit by a bus like you see on Hong Kong melodramas!)
And L. who died after so much pain. (Died in his sleep!)
And D. who died alone in the hospital with no one to claim his body for weeks. (Died with all his friends around him. Someone made a joke and everybody laughed and when the laughing and repetition of the punchline died down, D. had passed away with a smile; his mother cried for months!)

This is the way I know how to live and nobody has the power to fuck with my memories but me, so this body, baby, this body better play along.

Calculating the Velocity of Fabulousness

There are names for someone like Francis Lim Wee Meng:
Sister   Sissy   Queeny   Homo   Faggot   Bapok   Aqua

Francis Lim Wee Meng doesn't want to be called Wee Meng. He doesn't want to be called the state-preferred romanized Chinese of Ling Wei-Ming either. He wants to be called Francis. Just like the glamorous singer pop sensation chanteuse Francis Yip, star of 827 Remy Martin VSOP Cognac advertisements. Francis Yip, plump and frizzy haired, who's able to descend three flights of stairs in a tight sequined dress and four-inch stilettos without touching the banister, or looking at her feet, all the while singing "Big Spenda"... while being strangled by boa feathers.

Francis Lim Wee Meng is a bad queen, not like Ruben Wong. Ruben Wong got straight As, was on the debate team, the drama team, the Boy's Brigade, and represented the school in the state sponsored "Energy-Conservation Quiz." Ruben Wong got to wear his gold cheongsam onstage everytime there was a stage play where a female role was called for. Everybody said Ruben looked good in his gold cheongsam, his big bubble earrings, high heels, and makeup. Francis Lim Wee Meng was in the lower classes and no gold cheongsam, bubble earrings, high heels, or makeup could make Francis Lim Wee Meng's grade go up, not since he spent most of his time designing fabulous dresses in the margins of all his textbooks. Ruben Wong was bound for great things, everbody said; Francis Lim Wee Meng was bound for a bad sex change, everybody said.

If there was one day that Francis Lim Wee Meng and his friends lived for, it was the school's annual Music and Drama Night.

After school, the queens would take over one classroom, close all the windows, and give each other makeovers. Then, they would sashay across the concrete basketball court all the way to the auditorium (ignoring the catcalls and obscenities shouted at them) to watch the evening's performances, knowing full well that they were the best performance.

The first time I saw Francis Lim Wee Meng in a dress outside of school was on Bugis Street. He was with a group of his friends. All sashaying and teasing the tourists. (This was way back before the government bulldozed the entire alley where the drag queens lived and worked.) Francis Lim Wee Meng was wearing a yellow dress, a wig, heels, handbag. He had boobs made out of newspaper. I knew it was newspaper because I could see a small bit of it peeking through his bra. A group of marines were sitting nearby and one of them grabbed Francis Lim Wee Meng. Francis Lim Wee Meng laughed and tried to get away but a scuffle ensued and one of the marines pushed Francis Lim Wee Meng into a small dirty drain. The marines and tourists who saw this laughed and went back to their food that was getting cold on the tables set out under the

Attack of the Man-Eating Lotus Blossoms

nightlights and warm night sky.

Francis Lim Wee Meng started crying and his friends helped him out of the drain and briskly walked him out of the alley. Francis Lim Wee Meng's mascaraed tear-stained face saw me as he was walking out, and I saw him. We pretended that we did not know each other. I was in no mood to be nice to anyone anyway cos the man I was dating at that time had just beat the shit out of me and threatened to grind my face in with with a broken wine bottle.

Francis Lim Wee Meng and I have never said a word to each other even though we share a history of parks and cheap hotels. Mere geography to us.

Francis Lim Wee Meng knows a lot about my life because we both ended up one day in the park across Plaza Singapura cruising for men. Francis Lim Wee Meng saw me and I saw him but we didn't say a word to each other. We just pretended that we didn't know each other at all.

Francis Lim Wee Meng left with a strange-looking man. I saw them leave and enter his car. Francis Lim Wee Meng looked at me from the car window. I pretended not to see him. I left with someone to go to the shopping mall nearby to have sex in the bathroom on the fifth floor where there were no guards and the cleaners seldom came to wash the floor.

Two days later, the front page of the *New Straits Times* said that Francis Lim Wee Meng was found in a bathtub in a cheap hotel room off Bencoolen Street with a cord around his neck. Francis Lim Wee Meng was alive but in serious condition. The papers said it was a botched suicide attempt. Francis Lim Wee Meng lived to say that it was a botched suicide attempt. All I remember was thinking that the strange man could have picked me up and I would have gone with him.

Months later, I saw Francis Lim Wee Meng at the park again. We ignored each other again. Francis Lim Wee Meng has a scar on the left side of his ribcage. That's where my cousin and his friends bashed Francis Lim Wee Meng with a hockey stick one day after school.

One day a few years ago, after I left home and came to America, I could have sworn I saw Francis Lim Wee Meng on the street. One evening at a park, cruising, I saw someone who looked like Francis Lim Wee Meng. The person I saw looked at me as if he knew me as he was leaving with someone.

I called my mother recently to ask if she had heard anything about this guy I went to school with called Francis Lim Wee Meng. She said she wasn't sure if it was the same one but the papers reported a few years ago that someone that sounded like that got a sex change, got infected, got quarantined, and killed herself one evening in the wards. Slashed her wrists along the vein, not across. Do it right and nothing, no one, can save you even if they get to you in time. "Why are you so interested?" she asked me. "What has it got to do with you?"

Edge

Justin Chin
Attack of the Man-Eating Lotus Blossoms

Performance: May 26 & 27, 8 pm $7 general, $6 students, $5 members

"The Authentic Cultural Experience" as fetishized by a Karaoke Bar host, Margaret Mead on speed, psycho sex tour guide from hell, and a cooking show host from Planet PoMo

photo by Hiroko Nagao

The LAB is located at
1807 Divisadero Street in
San Francisco
For information and
reservations call:
(415)346-4063

Attack of the Man-Eating Lotus Blossoms
(1995-2000)

Looking back at these performances, I can't help but think of the possibilities, the stuff I could have done if I had the technology I now have—if I just had my iMac in 1995.

Attack... was an opportunity to put together several thematically linked vignettes to make a full show. It was a bit more ambitious than I had the gall or the resources to take on, but the younger me was so up for a challenge. There was a lot of media in the show: video, sound bits, recorded parts, and a *helluva* lot of slides.

One of the most fun gigs I ever had was doing the karaoke bit on Joan Jett Blakk's stage talk show in Berkeley. The venue regularly screened films so it was set up perfectly. There's something quite enlivening about an entire audience singing along to "I Will Survive" while footage of someone's penis being whipped, flogged, and poked with needles plays on a twenty-foot screen.

Pandora's Box... and *A(nthro)pology* came about in 1990 after I read an article published in the late *Christopher Street*. "Lust in the Mysterious East: Singapore" was as insipid and corny as its title suggests, and was written by living fossil/scholar Tobias "I Ate Someone's Liver Once" Schneebaum.
    It seems almost inconceivable that a gay publication, in 1990, would publish something so hackneyed, an article whose thinking was so outdated. But then, in 1990, when you walked into a bookstore or library and asked for a book about gay Asian (any sort of Asian, it's a big continent, pick any) themes, you weren't likely to get more than a couple of titles and a stack of *Oriental Guy* magazine. So perhaps an article about what makes the Singaporean gay under the age of twenty-five tick ($20 and the opportunity to gaze at a U.S. passport, apparently) written by a prominent anthropologist no less, must have seemed so fresh, so unexplored to the editors, who simply

could not resist.

I performed a version of *Food or Fuck*, using a modified version of the blood-letting act from *These Nervous Days*, at the Golden Ring Awards, a gala black-tie red-carpet event honoring Asian American actors, musicians, and other media artists.

When the organizers first contacted me about performing at the awards, I was dead chuffed about it, if a tad bewildered. I wrote them a very nice note saying, thank you but are you aware of the work I do? And if you want to rescind the invite, I won't be offended. They called back and said that they did indeed want me to perform.

The awards were held that year at Davies Symphony Hall, and among the artists honored were John Woo, Tia Carrere, and Russell Wong; the Rev. Jesse Jackson and Michelle Yeoh were slated to present. It was a big to-do.

We only had one small road-bump. After the rehearsal, the organizers asked if I would remove the word "fuck" from my piece. They feared that it would offend some of the audience. I thought about it and decided I would not. Not just because it was part of the language of the piece, or because it is so knee-jerk reactionary to be offended by the word "fuck." But also because I felt that any offense taken at the word "fuck" was stymied by the awards honoring director John Woo, whose work I adore, but is also unquestionably violent. A portrayal of violence and killing people, no matter how beautifully rendered, is still violence and people being killed, and the entertainment value of that should be more disturbing than using the word "fuck" in a passage describing sex tourism in Southeast Asia.

To their credit, the organizers gave it one last shot and then did not push any further on the subject.

For the performance, I was testing out a character affectionately referred to as the demon-possessed dim sum server. I wore a bitch-red cheongsam with the slit altered so that it went up to my waist on both sides, knee-high leather boots with fishnet stockings underneath, and my eyes were made up to have a dark raccoon-eye look, almost like a fetish mask, but drawn on. The performance had a recorded bit and a live spoken bit. During the recorded part, I used a syringe and drew blood out of my arm, then in the transition to the live

Attack of the Man-Eating Lotus Blossoms

part, I emptied the contents of the syringe over a bowl of steamed white rice, which I consumed as a coda to the piece.

***

A(nthro)pology

(A film/video loop of a smallish airplane flying in slight slow motion across the screen, in a diagonal arc from bottom to top, is rear projected. The performer stands behind the screen so only his silhouette, from shoulders upward, is seen. The text of the "interview" may be prerecorded, or the performer may choose to answer the questions live to a prerecorded question track, or have someone play the interviewer and dispense with recording devices altogether.

During the piece, the performer uses his silhouette to interact with the plane flying across the screen: Let the plane fly in one ear and out the other. Let the plane crash into eye. Or forehead. Or back of head. React differently each time plane passes through head. Make shadow puppets of animals with hands — rabbit and dog are easiest — and chase the plane. Wave goodbye; wave hello. Swat the plane as if it were a fly. Chase after the plane to eat it. Let the plane fly into open mouth.)

Perhaps we can start by describing him. I will not describe him. He shall remain as fictive as a page on a coloring book that one fills with what crayons one has. You want to know if he's attractive. You need to know if you want to forgive him, or to loathe him. **Then where shall we start?** Anywhere. Else. **What can you tell me?** He was on a fellowship named after a dead person with too much money and a fear of people not remembering his name. He was researching a book, or an article for a magazine. He was collecting evidence, specimens, documentation, testing various thesis. **Where do you fit in all these?** I was part of his work. I and everyone in the picture. I am not naïve enough to believe that I was the only savage in the garden. Thinking that, or believing that would be hopelessly sentimental, foolish, and incredibly bad science. **Yes, it would be bad science.** But the research was already faulty.

Justin Chin

Why do you say that? Codes, contexts, revision, all that crap. **Did he not understand the full picture? The frame within the frame? Could someone have not explained it to him?** I used to believe that my teddy bears came to life at night when I was asleep. I would lie still in my bed with the blanket pulled up right under my eyes and pretend to sleep. Then I'd peek and see if they moved. They always knew when to stop moving. **Interesting. So when he closed his eyes, when he went to sleep, did the "bears" actually move? What did they do?** The bears slept with him. At the foot of his bed. He should have made provisions for such holes in the research. **Did you ever catch the bears moving?** He had a friend, an acquaintance. A German man who lived in the room next to him at a hostel, a rooming house in Bangkok. This man was on the lam for some crime or another in Europe. He would bring young children back to his room and bathe them, keep them overnight. I always wondered if their parents missed them. They came in their school uniforms and left in their school uniforms in the morning. **Interesting. I'm looking at his notes and his articles, and apparently, he had some kind of...affection for you. Did he ever say he loved you?** Nobody ever loves anybody. Love and research. There are too many people that believe in love. But what they perceive to be love is merely a mistranslation. **I see... What was your relationship to him? With him?** He needed a show and I provided it. Object, speech. Object, speech. I undress and he takes it all and puts it into categories, indexes, cross-referencing to everything and everyone that came before me and will come after me and the results will benefit humankind who long to understand. **Did you lie to him? Deliberately sabotage his research, his life's work?** It is not enough to feign amazement at a toaster, to shriek when the "magic looking glass" is pulled out of the bag. A decade ago perhaps, that would have worked. Now the show is more subtle. **What show did you provide him?** The tie. That is a good example. I ask him to teach me how to put on a tie. His tie. His fat ugly poorly cut tie. It's not anything that a young boy in his hometown wouldn't ask an adult, but here in the heat, humidity, the unpronounceably named streets, there is more meaning to the act. **Yes, I remember the passage of the tie.** There is infinitely more meaning. His chubby hands around my neck, trying to work a cord, tie a knot around it.

Attack of the Man-Eating Lotus Blossoms

Read what you want into that gesture. **I see. Any others?** Hair has always been a perennial favorite, though it has become far too popular lately. Still, it matters how it is used. The less imaginative ones simply fawn over it all. Beards, an unimpressive smattering of chest hair, the comb-over. **His work does speak a bit about the fascination with Western hair.** He had a friend who had a book of pubic hairs clipped from boys he had known, he had picked up. It's a mystical book. A few others have alluded to it but few have ever seen it. **That wasn't mentioned. Perhaps it could not be corroborated. There is something that I must ask you. It is the main thrust of his work.** He longs to hear how much I wanted to be white. To be like him and others like him. But I cannot and I have never had such longings. I never thought that I was white. **But did he ask you if you ever wanted to be white?** Yes, he was following a pattern in his research. **And you said?** Here is what he wrote in what he thought was to be his private diary: "Had a strange dream. I was Chinese. I spoke the language and understood everything about being Chinese. I ate the food that I had never dared try before (even as adventurous as I pretend to be!). It is a strange feeling being something else. I am having some deep musings about the theories of skin, color, race, and [here, the writing is illegible].... I need to rethink some of these before I commit them to paper. I need to see more, to understand this work I'm doing. It is important work. [Here, two sentences are deleted.] C. has been a great help and he is indeed attractive, intelligent, though perhaps a bit young in his thoughts. I can't remember if any of the boys were in the dream though and this interests me. In all, it was a beautiful dream and I wished I never woke from it. I only hope that it shall return." **Yes, I know his journals well. Do you feel anything, knowing that you misled him on something that was his whole life's work?** We're dealing with the trafficking of lies, nothing more. **Perhaps you misread his work.** Because there is an essential lie that we are led to believe in. **And that lie is?** "...[T]hat beneath our skin, we are all the same...." **You are citing him.** If that were true, we wouldn't be doing so many things that we are led to do. That beneath and beyond the skin, and between the layers of skin, each stripped of color into trans-lucence as it slouches toward blood, everything we are held to be is still inscribed on that skin, that thing that holds our flesh in place. **You contradict his ideas yet confirm them in some ways, I believe.** There are only two ways that Asian skin can actually become permanently white: fungus and decom-position. There are other methods, of course, bleaching, powders with mercuric oxide that strip away the skin. But these methods are uncertain. **Is certainty the only factor here?** Fire. Unlike black skin that turns white with third-degree burns, Asian skin only turns a dour red. **He would have loved to hear this.** White skin turns black. **What did you want, or expect, from him?** I wanted less than what my peers wanted, much less. They were shooting for blue jeans, consumer products, ideals of Hollywood romance. The most ambitious ones aimed for a green-card sponsor. **And you wanted?** If I told you, it would disappear like a birthday wish whispered into a confidant's ear too soon. A waste of the original breath taken to blow out all those candles. Might as well save it all for the final sigh. **So what did you get out of it all?** What did I get out of it? Possibly, the same things you are getting out of this.

Mis·Translations

(*Try to have a pole, the kind strippers use, or a column or pillar, one can't be so picky with these things. The "translations" are performed as a go-go boy, the type found, or the type we think we'll find, in Asia. Except that the performer is fully clothed. In fact, he's put on gloves and an anorak as well.*

The English bits of the "translation" are prerecorded; if you can find someone with a good English-speaking accent [the networks use Canadians, I'm told] that'll be excellent.)

How much is that pineapple? **Berapa harga nanas itu?**
One dollar and fifty cents. **Seringgit lima puluh sen.**
That is expensive. **Itu mahal.**
May I make a bargain? **Bolehkah saya awar?**
Yes, of course! **Tentu boleh.**
What is the fixed price? **Berapa harga pastinya?**
One ringgit, Sir. **Serinngit, Tuan.**
Can I get it for less? **Tak boleh kurang lagi?**
That is already reasonable. **Iti sudah patut.**

Attack of the Man-Eating Lotus Blossoms

Etc. Etc. Etc.
In 1970, United Features allowed Popeye to be translated into Chinese. In one strip, Popeye and Swee'Pea go to an island that Popeye has purchased. Translated back into English, the strip goes:

Popeye: What a beautiful kingdom. I am king, I am president, I can be anything I want to be.
Swee'Pea: What about me?
Popeye: You can be the crown prince.
Swee'Pea: If I'm going to be anything, I want to be president.
Popeye: Your tone of voice is bold for someone who is merely a baby.
Swee'Pea: But there's only two of us in the whole country!
Popeye: My island is a democratic country. Everyone can vote.
Swee'Pea: Everyone? There's just the two of us. I'll run for election too.
Popeye: Let me make my election speech. Fellow countrymen...
Swee'Pea: Not bad.
Popeye: Fellow countrymen, you must not vote for Swee'Pea.
Swee'Pea: Hey, what's the big idea!

It goes on, but somehow, you can't help but think that something was lost in the translation.

Have you ever seen cockfighting? **Pernahkan anda melihat laga ayam?**
It is a cruel act. **Itu perbuatan yang kejam.**
This egg will be fried. **Teloh ini digoreng.**
Brokenhearted. **Pata hati.**
Let's eat! **Mari kita makan!**

Getting to Know You
I'm supposed to do this bit naked, or in a jockstrap at least. But I decided not to. Friends and onlookers advise me otherwise. They tell me: Taking your clothes off is a political act! It offers the queer body as the exquisite sacrifice to the vultures of the conservative backlash on the human body in the 20th century. Taking your clothes off will strike a blow against stereotypes of Asians as unsexual and shameful of their bodies. Taking your clothes off will place you firmly in one of the most time-

honored traditions of gay theater and gay performance. Taking your clothes off in the age of AIDS will be a powerful statement of reclaiming the body from the ugly talons of disease and shame. Taking your clothes off will get you offers to go on dates, the oh-so-hip columnists in the queer rags will love you. You will become a cultural icon as your performance stylings in the nude will amaze onlookers like a ten-car accident on the 101.

But they don't understand.
This body doesn't just belong to me. The Queer Chinese Body belongs to the collective notions of family, culture, race. The diaspora wants it to be a bridge to homelands long gone, never remembered, just left. The homeland owns a significant number of shares in it. The queer bits belong to the collective good of that big discotheque called Gay Rights (Free entry before Affirmative Action with this coupon, bring more IDs if you're colored.). I have to keep this body intact in all ways so I can work my split shift in the Rainbow factory, turning out consumer durables for the new Queer Age. I'll need this body intact for the coming Rice dream, the final coming of the new Asia (no longer just a big-ass continent!).

Keeping my clothes on is a political act. It stands against the incessant need to create positive and unblemished images of strength and power, against essentialism, even as these images reinscribe patriarchal and colonial ideals of power.

Keeping my clothes on is a political act and that's why I'm not taking my clothes off.

And besides, I feel really really flabby these days.

The servant washed Mr. Smith's clothes. **Orang gagi itu mencucci pakaian Encik Smith.**
All my mangoes have been stolen! **Habis buah manggaku dicuri!**

Attack of the Man-Eating Lotus Blossoms

Happier Talk

Onscreen — either a projection or on monitors — "Happy Talk" from the movie South Pacific *plays. It is the scene where Bloody Mary tries to get her young charge and the GI to fall in love. The song is supposed to do the trick.*

Sitting cross-legged in a sarong, the performer performs along to the images onscreen, perfectly mimicking the action, especially the hand-gestured sign language that the character uses to illustrate how sweet and lovely the song is.

After a few minutes, at least after the first verse, the performer stands and unknots the sarong which he holds up and uses as a screen. Then, making a big show of it, he urinates into a tall cocktail glass. The performer picks up the glass and brings it to his mouth as if he is going to drink it, but stops short. Frowning, he puts the glass down. Then he produces an ice bucket seemingly out of nowhere. He puts ice cubes into the glass and then decorates the glass with fruit and tropical umbrellas and a funny twirly straw.

Holding it up for the audience's approval, the performer then proceeds to drink. If the movie on the screen is playing the part where the Yat is splashing in the water, the performer performs along by blowing bubbles in the glass; the mood of this action should match the gleeful splashing onscreen.

Pandora's Box of Shrimp Chow-Fun

I. Ingredients

Inauthentic Recipe	**Authentic Recipe**
1/2 pound shrimp	半镑虾
1 cup bean sprouts	一杯子豆芽
1 stalk spring onion	春天葱
1 or 2 slices of fresh ginger root	2 片式姜根
1/2 medium-sized yellow onion	半媒体黄色葱
1 tablespoon cornstarch	1 把大汤匙 米面粉
2 tablespoons soy sauce	2 把大汤匙酱油
1 tablespoon sherry	1 把大汤匙雪利酒
oil, salt	油, 盐

Justin Chin

A Story:
Let me tell you a story. It is an old story that my grandmother told me. Actually, my grandmother's great-grandmother who died after my grandmother's grandmother told her (my grandmother's great-grandmother) this story and so it has been passed down. It's supposedly true, but who really knows. The originator is said to be centuries back. My grandmother's great-grandmother told her the story when my grandmother was in a wheelbarrow traveling to another city because their village was wrecked by famine, huge insects, and a tornado. But my grandmother left her hometown eventually by boat and settled here, where she married my grandfather. The story her grandmother told her was also told to my mother and her sister, my aunties. Anyhow, I can't remember the story quite that well, but it's a good story with a good message.

II. Method

   1. Bring a large quantity of water to a boil. Do not add salt or oil. (Diagram 1)

Dried Wheat Flour Noodles are sold in one pound packages in foot lengths. The noodles imported from Hong Kong sometimes contain fish or fish roe flavorings and are much better than the domestic made ones. Ignore the English label on the imported package that proclaims "Imitation Noodle"; these are the best kind of noodles and the label is merely the manufacturers conforming to U.S. Food and Drug Administration laws.

   2. Cook Fun noodles to taste. Run cooked noodles under cool water. (Diagram 2)

Attack of the Man-Eating Lotus Blossoms

Diagram 1.

"Gone is the great sewage stench that lifted on occasion to reveal exotic smells of silks and damasks, lustrous Oriental fabrics, incense, perfumes and spices redolent with fragrances that turn the mind to Araby and Persia, to India, China and Mongolia."

(Attach picture of Margaret Mead in Diagram 1 box.)

Diagram 2.

"It was in Singapore in the 1950s that I had become enamored of Eastern men and had indulged myself with Chinamen and Malays, with Sikhs, Tamils, and Bengalis."

(Attach picture of atomic bomb at Hiroshima in Diagram 2 box.)

3. Shell and devein shrimp. Mince ginger root. Combine with cornstarch, soy sauce, and sherry. Add to shrimp and toss to coat. Heat oil. Add shrimp and stir-fry until almost cooked. (Diagram 3)

(Quote) Modern air travel has brought the whole of Asia literally to our doorstep, no matter where we may live. The twentieth-century world has shrunk astonishingly: access to once-distant and remote places is now limited only by the size of our purses and perhaps, our capacity for adventure.

Along with easy access has come a new awareness of Oriental culture and a surge of Western interest in Oriental food and Oriental cooking. (End Quote)

Justin Chin

identity as product
[Special Combo Meal Deal: Homosexuality, Ethnicity + Large Fries & Medium Soft Drink. $4.95. NO SUBSTITUTIONS PLEASE.]

Diagram 3.

"I had pressed forward every opportunity for enjoyment with young men. In Persia once, a handsome youngster of fourteen offered for sale at $25, a slave I might have purchased for life.... Everywhere I went, men sought other men, some for money, some for love, some for time with a stranger."

(Attach picture of aircraft carriers on stopover in Southeast Asia here or picture of the military encouraging the economy of Southeast Asia in Diagram 3 box.)

Diagram 4.

"The essential elements of bawdiness and licentiousness were gone...no one could approach Singapore today with its sterile antiseptic appearance and envision those real life fantasies I had acted out, in which I let myself go all out and fuck in elegant surroundings and drink Singapore Slings while seated in rattan chairs.... There had never been a problem then finding young men eager to spend the night for a buck."

(Attach picture of your first pick from Oriental Brides Galore *Nov. 2000 issue in Diagram 4 box.)*

Attack of the Man-Eating Lotus Blossoms

Tradition
Huang:
"Twadeeshon. Twatit`tion. Tra-lalala-diction. Tra-nee-sion. Thra-dee-shin."
> (Verbatim Transcript. Interview 6/9/93.)

    4. Add more oil and salt and cook bean sprouts and green onion. (Diagram 4)

(Quote) There is no culture in the world that is more obsessed with food than the Chinese, and it seems to have always been that way. When the Chinese are not involved in the actual preparation of a meal, they are talking about the next meal. (End Quote)

identity as map
everything behind my skin defines me
everything beyond my skin I discover
someone else's fur
someone else's bones
someone else's blood
someone else's semen
things I take in my mouth
things I take in my ass
things I take home

    5. Cover pan and let vegetables cook in their own steam until they are soft. (Diagram 5)

Diagram 5:

"There was something captivating about the young men around. Looking at their slender bodies, without waistlines, produced a profound yearning inside me that didn't go away. They are not skinny, but are hard and supple and strong. I like their quickness of mind, their enthusiasm and willingness to learn."

(Attach picture of your favorite Asian design motif, or, water buffalo in Diagram 5 box.)

(Quote) In order to better understand the integral role that food plays in the culture, we need to admit that a culture cooks in a particular way because of the way it thinks. (End Quote)

identity as representation
    speak as
    speakas
    speak as whole
    speak ass

Powerful
Xiao Ming:
"Powerful? Yes, I believe that Tide...Tide with Bleach. Bleach Alternative is the most powerful. Er...you see...it was...I think it was two years ago, yes, two years ago when I got my nipple pierced and they hit a vein and...like it took two days for the blood to reach the surface. And like, it was...er...I was sleeping and the next day, I got up, when I got up, there was blood all over my sheets and shirt. And I thought, *Okay, might as well throw it out*, but then I thought, *Maybe I'll soak them first*. So I used Tide and it all came out. Still have those sheets. (laughs)."
                              (Verbatim Transcript. Interview 3/4/93)

    6. Add noodles and stir-fry until sauce covers the noodles. (Diagram 6)

(Quote) The Chinese preoccupation with food is not due to the fact that they have known starvation. Many cultures have passed through starving times but have never reached the culinary heights attained by the Chinese. Nor is their fascination with food due to their willingness to try anything and everything, though they have. (End Quote).

identity as LEGO blocks
    Some people can make the helicopter, the airplane, the brontosaurus as pictured on the side of the box. Some people just make solid chunks and throw them at their siblings. It all depends on a bit of imagination and of course, the types and number of blocks you have.

Attack of the Man-Eating Lotus Blossoms

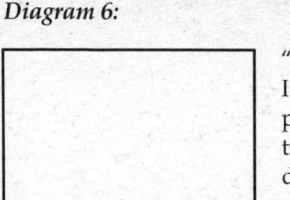

Diagram 6:

"There was an odd taste to his penis I could not identify. He changed positions constantly, prolonging time between orgasms, and was a delight to be with."

(Attach action still from Jean-Claude Van Damme's Oriental oeuvre in Diagram 6 box.)

Exotic
Trac:
"Please to repeat after me:
    'Is that a toaster?'
    'May I have my meat medium, please?'
    'Is that a Hoover?'
    'Wow!'"
(Verbatim Transcript. Interview 8/9/93. Interviewee is a language instructor by profession. He plans to be a flight attendant.)

    7. Serve immediately while hot. (Diagram 7)

(Quote) Even Asian-style cooking requires moderation in eating. It is the key in any cuisine. [In the library copy of this book, some previous reader had underlined this last sentence three times and written the word "True" in the margin.] Eating less of everything will help you lose weight. And maintain control of yourself. (End Quote)

identity as bondage
    "There's nothing I enjoy more than to be tied up and unmercifully fucked."

Culture
"The Chinese Barber" first appeared in *The Threepenny Review*; "Stitches" in *The Little Magazine*; "Ordinary Chinese People" and "Robbed" in *The Asian/Pacific American Journal*; "A Nice Chinese Girl" in *Bakunin*; "Chinese Movie" in *The Turtle Creek*

Justin Chin

Review; "Open House" and "Cultural Revolution" in *The Kenyon Review*....

(Acknowledgments to C—— R——, N—— W——, P—— P——, 1994)

Sample Question #1:
Is N—— W—— a) Chinese?
b) Non-Chinese?
c) Good Chinese?
d) Bad Chinese?
e) Asian?
f) Asian American?

What you eat is important. It's almost like a cultural marker that tells an observer where you are; it places you in the cultural epoch. When archaeologists discovered the almost perfectly preserved remains of the Ice-Man or The Body Entombed in Lava, they sent a probe into the corpses' intestines and colon to pick out the remains in order to examine what people ate in the ages before microwavable nouvelle cuisine. They found berries, nuts, and some fat in the Ice-Man. Predictable—but it wasn't his fault; he did live in a perpetual blizzard and you just know how damn difficult it is to get a good Chicken Kiev in a blizzard, so I'm sure he just made do. In The Body Entombed in Lava, they found some grain (they said polenta) and little bones, perhaps wingtips of grouse. In the picture of The Body Entombed in Lava, his right hand is clenched in a strange manner. His finger and thumb meet delicately and his other fingers are spread fan-like. What the scientist did not realize was that The Body Entombed in Lava was daintily eating when he died. How horrible; imagine the talk about *that* dinner party. "And then Noshka started telling that interminable story about the crocodiles in the Nile *again*. If it wasn't for that scrumptious feast, but then, that beastly volcano erupted and disturbed the whole party! That's it, that's the last time *I'm* going to a do at the Sumerians."

Attack of the Man-Eating Lotus Blossoms

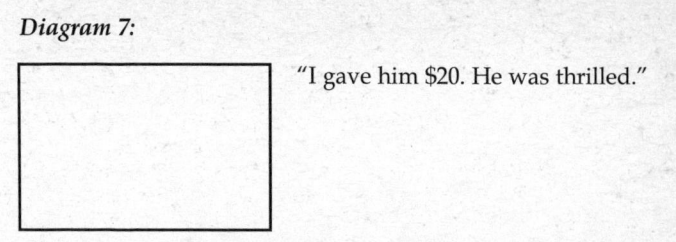

Diagram 7:

"I gave him $20. He was thrilled."

(Attach – no staples please – brochure for Asian sex tour in Diagram 7 box.)

(How shall we end this but with) *The Utopian Sense of Shrimp Chow Fun:*
1. The shrimp is firm and its flavor is not overpowered by the sauce.
2. The noodles do not all separate, some should clump together in a thick slab.
3. It is not too oily.
4. It leaves a pleasant aftertaste.
5. You want some more.

THIS DISCLAIMER LIMITS OUR LIABILITY: Do not attempt this recipe unless properly supervised. The author/performer takes no responsibility for any injury, illness, or dissatisfaction from trying out the recipe(s) contained herein.

NOTES/SOURCES:
Quotes cited to diagrams are from:
- "Lust in the Mysterious East: Singapore" by Tobias Schneebaum. *Christopher Street*, Issue 145, Vol 13. No. 1., 1990.
- *Chinese Technique: An Illustrated Guide to the Fundamental Techniques of Chinese Cooking* by Ken Hom and Harvey Steiman. Simon & Schuster, 1981.
- *The Frugal Gourmet Cooks 3 Ancient Cuisines: China, Greece & Rome* by Jeff Smith. William Morrow & Co., 1989.
- *Weight Control & Asian Foods* by Kay Shimizu. Japan Publishing Co., 1975.
- *Oriental Cookbook* by Priya Wickramasinghe. Dent & Sons, 1982.
- *Oriental Cooking with Madame Wu: The Yin/Yang Cookbook for Health & Balance* by Madame Wu. Denton, 1985.

Justin Chin

Happy Fun Karaoke Time

The following songs are offered as a choice for a karaoke moment.

1. "I'd Do Anything for Love (But I Won't Do That)," (originally recorded by Meatloaf)
2. "I Will Survive," (originally recorded by Gloria Gaynor)
3. "I Will Always Love You," (originally recorded by Dolly Parton, though Linda Ronstadt did a version of it on her *Prisoner in Disguise* album. The most recognized version though is the Whitney Houston cover.)

The video accompanying each song features scenes of heavy S/M, genital mutilation, and genital torture. This is best done with a large full-screen projection, though several TV monitors would do.

An Exotic Folk Tale from Far Away (Based on a True Story)

(The performer walks in, he's wearing slippers which slap against his soles. He sits on a small stool and reads from a big story book in that Romper Room/Children's Television voice.

Overhead, images of puckered sphincters are projected while story is read.)

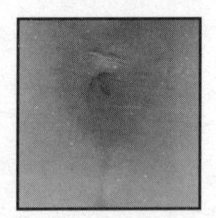

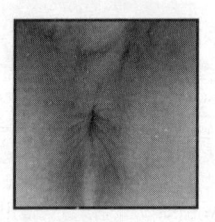

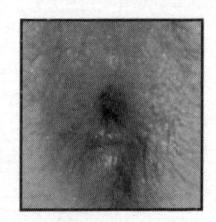

Hello, Boys and Girls. It's time for a story! You like stories, don't you? Today's story is special. It comes a land far far away called Malaysia. Can you say "Malaysia"? Very good!

In Malaysia, there lived a boy named Wang, who dreamed of going to America. Wang worked in the padi fields helping his

Attack of the Man-Eating Lotus Blossoms

Mummy and Daddy grow yummy rice. Wang hated working in the padi field. It was hot and he had to stand in water all day. He hated bending down and there were so many mosquitoes that bit him.

Wang was a lonely boy. He missed his brother who died of polio a year ago. Wang worked very hard and tried to save his money so he could go to America, but it was too expensive. One day, on his birthday, his Mummy and Daddy surprised him with a wonderful present. Can you guess what it was, boys and girls? No, it wasn't a brand-new rice cooker! No, it wasn't a Nintendo 64 System! No, it wasn't Paula Abdul's new album! What? No, it wasn't a series of tetanus booster shots!?! It was a round-trip plane ticket to America!

Wang couldn't wait to get to America so he could eat hamburgers, see Mickey Mouse in real life, and go to Aerosmith concerts and hear them perform their hits, "Cryin'," "Walk This Way," "Amazing," "Love in an Elevator," "Crazy," "Livin' on the Edge," "Janie's Got a Gun," "Rag Doll," "Deuces Are Wild," and "Dude (Looks Like a Lady)." *What an exciting adventure*, he thought.

Wang boarded the small aeroplane with many other people: students, families, and businessmen! It was really cramped and the flight was oversold and many people could not get on the plane, but everyone was so excited! They were flying across the big blue ocean on their way…to America!

Soon, they reached America! The small aeroplane landed in a big airport. Wang got his passport and visas ready. He had to go through customs and immigration. Can you say "customs and immigration"? It's a big word, but I know you can say it. Good! If you are having trouble saying it, ask your Mummy or Daddy or your U.S. Immigration Sponsor to help you.

But the nice immigration officers stopped Wang and many of the people on the plane. The officers heard a tip that many Malaysians were coming to America on tourist visas and then not returning to their own countries. No, they were staying in America to become Illegal Aliens. Can you say "Illegal Alien"?

Justin Chin

Very good! It's a big scary word, I know, and if you're having touble saying it, ask your local state legislator to help you!

So after detaining the travelers in jail for ten days, Wang and his friends were finally asked to go back to their own country. Wang was so disappointed. Now he would never know what the dude who looked like a lady looked like.

But it's okay, because even if Wang can't go to America, America can still come to Wang. Yes, many American battleships and aircraft carriers go to Malaysia to visit and relax in the sun. The Malaysian locals just love the American visitors!

Do you want to go to a foreign country, children? Well, you can! With your imagination! And if you don't have any imagination, you can still ask your Mummy or Daddy to take you to a restaurant that serves food from that country; it's almost like being there but you don't have to deal with the squat toilets! And you don't have to speak the language. Wouldn't that be so much fun, children?

(Alternate Staging:
The whole story is prerecorded in that Romper Room/Children's Television *voice. The performer wears slippers. In darkness or in very dim light, you can hear the slippers slapping against the soles of the feet. There is a string of lightbulbs beside the wall socket.*

The lightbulbs (ten-sixteen lightbulbs will do) are strung together on a single wire, ending with one small appliance bulb. If 25-watt lightbulbs are used, the effect is nice and warm; if 40-watt and above bulbs are used, the effect will be quite intense.

The string of lightbulbs is plugged into the socket. The performer takes the last bulb and places it in his mouth. Then, crawling, he laboriously drags the string of lights to the middle of the space. On his hands and knees, the performer suddenly starts thrashing about as if he were having an epileptic fit or a demon possession. This is done until the story ends. If the performer thrashes with enough vim, a few of the bulbs should hopefully shatter or pop.)

Attack of the Man-Eating Lotus Blossoms

Missionary Positions

(The performer strips down to his underwear and proceeds to smear Vaseline over his exposed flesh. The performer reaches for a gorgeous evening bag [sequined or beaded will be wonderful] or a fabulous makeup bag that is sitting nearby. The performer opens the bag dramatically. The bag is filled with raw rice. The performer proceeds to scoop the rice out of the bag with his hands and smear it onto his Vaseline-covered flesh. Try to cover as much ground as possible.

That done, the performer finds pauses in the texts/speech where he shakes himself like a hula-school drop-out, or a wet beagle – the shake is spasming, staccato, a violent but controlled burst. If done correctly, the rice should spray across the performance space, hitting the floor with a grainy clatter.)

The person that showed up some thirty years ago to save our poor souls was a British missionary named Mr. Kirton. Then, the town was still a small sleepy little place, and he immediately got a loan from the missions to buy a small plot of land where he started a little chapel.

Mr. Kirton dated Miss Lee (who played the organ on Sundays) and Miss Kok (who taught Sunday School to preschoolers). After a few years, Mr. Kirton married Miss Lee. Miss Lee became Mrs. Kirton and played the organ every Sunday until her diabetes laid her up, got her legs gangrenous, and they had to be amputated.

When my mom told me that Mrs. Kirton had her legs amputated, I knew that for weeks she and the other ladies, all nurses, had continually advised them on how to best convalesce, cautioning them about gangrene setting in. But Mr. Kirton said it was best to listen to the doctor. Perhaps what he was really saying was, *What do you dusky natives know about medicine? I'll trust my expatriate doctor trained overseas, thank you very much.* I told my mom my thoughts, and she said I "was evil."

Mr. Kirton was an amateur entomologist. He had a whole storeroom full of wooden boxes with glass plates. Inside, there were little butterflies, carefully pinned and labeled. The King Monarch, Swallowtail, etc., etc.

Entomology is perhaps the most sadistic profession. Taken as a hobby, the cruelty is magnified ten-fold. Here are all these beautiful butterflies that are netted, gassed, and pinned to a soft board—the price of beauty, of having intensely colored wings. This was the man who had come to save our native souls.

Mrs. Kirton died fourteen years ago. The remaining Kirtons moved to a different town. Miss Kok still teaches Sunday School to preschoolers.

On my mother's side, there were missionaries. I've heard of a great-(great?)grandfather who was a missionary and traveled up and down the peninsula saving souls until he caught leprosy and had to stay at home wrapped in heavy coats, even in the equatorial heat, until he died. Church was very much a part of my family life, even though my mother married outside the faith. Once, she said she had righted herself with God for marrying a non-Christian. Eventually, of course, my dad converted to make everyone happy, but he still worshipped a false god: Golf.

I got to know about the devil real early and he was very real. My grandmother had lived in a haunted house in Changi once, and she would often tell me stories of how she would see ghosts giggling in the corner and in my mind I imagined a fluffy Shmoo-like ghost, not unlike Casper, in the corner.

I really don't know much about my grandfather because he died when I was very young and all that was left of him were yellowed photographs on dressing tables and all his Bibles that were stored on a small shelf near my bed. Each Bible had the title page inscribed with his name or my grandmother's name and a bible verse. His handwriting was long, scrawly, and very ornate.

My mom occasionally asks if I'm still going to worship. I always lie, I say, "Once in a while." She knows I'm bluffing, but she pretends to be satisfied.

The other day, I was on the subway and this Chinese man asks for directions. He wants to go to Chinatown. I give him the directions, drudging out the Chinese that I hadn't used in a long time. He is glad that a youngster can still speak the language, even though not as well as I once could. "I understand more than I can speak these days," I tell him.

Attack of the Man-Eating Lotus Blossoms

"You remind me of my students," he says. He tells me that he was a principal in southern China on the China-Vietnam border. When the communists took over, he lost his job and separated from his family, became a refugee, ending up in missions and camps across Thailand, and eventually was sent to the United States. He starts to get teary-eyed. I say something vaguely consoling. He sighs heavily and says, "How shameful to be Chinese in this place." He gives me his card and tells me to come and see him sometime. He works as an assistant pastor at a Chinese church in Alameda.

Food or Fuck
If the world has seen America through the movies, I imagine how the world has seen me.

If America has seen my homeland through the movies, I imagine how America has seen me.

On Memorial Day two years ago, a telephone solicitor calls me up and asks me for money for some mumbled veterans fund. I do not recall what made me behave the way I did. I said, "A bunch of soldiers go to the Third World and kill a bunch of people who look like me and I'm supposed to help them because they can't sleep?"

The has-been actress on the telly plumps pity with a side of Christian do-good. Her red fingernails rest on the knobby head of a belly-bloated child, even as the promise of the spilled semen of green cards and Amex holidays slashes its way across the Third World.

Even as the gay community clamors to join the military. Even as the military offers one of the few solutions a poor queer can get to find the yellow brick road to the IKEA commercial at the end of the rainbow, where Melissa Etheridge serenades you while you fall in love with the closest approximation of yourself, a drag queen in Malaysia bleeds to death after a group of soldiers hacks off his penis to teach him a lesson.

Even as GIs and soldiers go on R&R in the sunny Third World, screwing their way into the psyche of a queen named Exotica, a sixteen-year-old boy dies because of the infection caused by the sex toy that shatters in his rectum, shoved there by his Big Daddy, who cries and moves on to the next one.

Even as AIDS inches further into wounds of the Third World, the AIDS-infected flight attendant lives out the rest of his life in Bangkok screwing without a condom and living out his dream of spreading his love to a bevy of beautiful boys.

Go ahead and plumb the Third World for your sense of spirituality, your fuck-me-all Godhead fix. Fuck as many colored folks as you want and rest easy in your futon feeling that you're making an affirmative gesture in the civil rights movement.

If America has seen me through my cuisine, I imagine how I would taste. On the days when I've been the hero, the monster, the slut, the piece of shit, some other permutation of myself.

My history, my past in my homeland, my life within my borders, does not just belong to me. On the day when I am taken by the early spit of my secret dulling, when nothing is as light as my unbearable heart, and nothing is as heavy as my untamable guts.

If I have seen myself through the movies, I imagine how I have seen myself.

I'm tired of explaining how it feels.

Son of South Pacific
Sunday. Last day of January 1993. It is the anniversary of the Tet Offensive. The Super Bowl is on at the Rose Bowl in Pasadena. The Ted Turner–owned channel is playing *South Pacific* and *Flower Drum Song* back-to-back all day. Michael Jackson is performing at the half-time special of the game. It is Johnny Rotten's birthday.

In *South Pacific*, Nurse Nellie, played by Mitzi Gaynor, shows Emile, the French planter, a clipping from a newspaper from her hometown in Little Rock, Arkansas. "Ensign Nellie

Attack of the Man-Eating Lotus Blossoms

Forbush, Arkansas' own Florence Nightingale," Emile reads. At the time, *South Pacific* was released, another image was carried in newspapers across the country. It was of fifteen-year-old Elizabeth Eckford trying to enter Little Rock's Central High School and being prevented from doing so by the Arkansas National Guard and a mob of jeering whites.

I return home to visit. My grandmother is loading the washing machine and I overhear her ask my mother why my clothes have that funny raw lambmeat smell; she deduced that it is the smell of America. She tells me my brother's clothes had a similar smell when he came back from England.

The King and I received a large revival during the '60s, the years of the wars and conflicts in Vietnam. Many should have seen the connections but few reviewers did. Perhaps the notions of a childlike Asian leader welcoming Western intervention and traditional Oriental culture yielding gracefully to Americanized notions of progress were some sort of comfort in the face of a war. And we need comforts in time of war.

Do we? That would depend on who's doing the warring on whom.

Back home, we used to look to the West for ideas of how to be queer. We want to know just what to do and how to do it beautifully.

When I was a young queer, first coming to America, I was picked up by a guy on the street, we went to his home, and he sucked my dick while *The Times of Harvey Milk* played on the TV.

I'm trying to work out the contradictions.

Where Asian values are a $1 Singapore Sling; and a good deal on those Seiko watches. Where color and borders and difference are consumed faster and with as much passion as takeout.

I'm trying to work out the contradictions.

And all I'm left with is a cloud. The smell of raw lambmeat.

JUSTIN CHIN
--in--
HOLY SPOOK

@ Dixon Place, 258 Bowery (1/2 block below Houston)   10:30 p.m.   8 Dollars
Friday 26 July, 1996 (with Eileen Myles)
Saturday 27 July, 1996 (with Jack Shamblin
For info, call: 219-3088

Holy Spook (1995-2000)

The beginning of *Holy Spook* is in no way a rip on Amy Tan. There are more than enough people rancorously and gleefully pooping on her already. Much of which, I might add, is wholly unwarranted. Rather, it's a poke at the sort of audience who come to expect, and in some cases, demand, the sentimental trappings of a particular kind of ethnic narrative.

In the Asian American milieu, that involves being eternally caught between two cultures and having tearful frays over it; wacky mix-ups, hilarious misunderstandings, and the bonsai-sized ruckus caused by this cultural dislocation or simply by misinterpretations; a supreme trauma or hardship that is valiantly overcome with a great show of strength (silent, brooding) and character (stoic); wise and Confucian-like teachings handed down from generation to generation; and everything—from toenail clippings to cumulonimbus clouds—is just dripping with metaphors of Deeper Eastern Meaning.

If gay, add coming-out story, and the initially hostile parents who eventually yield to their filial yoke. If you're ambitious, you can add the Best Drag Queen Friend (who may or may not get gay-bashed) or the guy with AIDS (who will surely die most heroically and immaculately).

Anything that deviates too much from this grid is snubbed as "inauthentic" or "westernized." Sentimentality is based on what you already know or think you know, a writer friend of mine once said.

There is nothing wrong with expecting or demanding something, some specific payoff, from the art, but that's different from demanding it from the artist.

Bare lightbulbs are one of my most favorite props.

In an earlier version of *Holy Spook*, I had a number of lightbulbs hanging at shoulder-to-head level, and while performing the text, I tried to break the bulbs with a hammer that I swung (always in the upstage direction, of course). The hammer had to be held in a very specific way and swung in a specific arc in order for the hammer head to hit its target squarely; this action done repeatedly puts a considerable strain on the upper body, and when that part of the performance is done, the strain is very clearly felt, sometimes even seen, on the body of the performer.

The lightbulb had to be hit with a certain force and at a certain angle before it would shatter. And when it did, it was so gorgeous: there was that spark, that pop, that sound of glass fragments and splinters as they hit the ground, the reflective glints they give off as they fly through the air, and the sudden decrease of light in the room. But when the bulb was struck and did not break, it merely picked up momentum, sending it spinning and swinging with more vim, making it even harder to crack. Then there was the sheer mess to clean up afterwards. Plus the jittery and distracted audience terrified glass splinters would come hurling at them. It was a right decision to mothball that gesture.

Of all my work, *Holy Spook* is the one that has been performed the most.

***

(Darkness; the performer lights a match. This section is performed lit by matchlight only. When the match burns out, the performer lights another match, then another....)

This Is Not The Joy Luck Club

My grandmother keeps a secret. She keeps a secret so deep inside of her that the pain of her arthritis is nothing compared to it. My grandmother and her sisters get together every weekend for a three-day marathon session of gambling and little snacks, gossip and one-upmanships comparing how each other's children and grandchildren are doing, who's doing better than whom, who's gotten into trouble. Nothing delights one of the old ladies more than the knowledge that one of their grandnephews or nieces is bringing shame upon the family, which could range anywhere from sheer rudeness to a grown-up to giving up piano lessons to interracial dating to getting bad grades at school.

Once, I asked my mother if she ever wondered what the old ladies were gossiping about us, about me. Leave them

Attack of the Man-Eating Lotus Blossoms

alone, my mother says. She tells me that this weekend session is especially important to my grandmother. In order to keep a secret, she has to find others to tell. That is the function of gossip. Family time is important to her, because of the losses she suffered in her long lifetime. One of her sisters committed suicide to flee a loveless marriage. Years ago, during the Japanese Occupation, grandma had to flee her village in the Southern Province of China; on her two-week-long trek to the harbors, she was forced to abandon her youngest child, my mom's younger sister, wrapped in her pink swaddling clothes with baby prints of spring flowers in a padi field, a pair of jade earrings and a jade bracelet carefully tucked into the baby's nappy. We do not know if that relative is alive or dead.

Oh, wait a minute, that's not me. That's *The Joy Luck Club*.

(The performer screws a lightbulb into live-wired socket. The bulb lights up abruptly. The effect is entirely different from a bulb that has simply been switched on.)

Sorry.
That just seems to keep happening these days.

But now that we've broken the Fourth Wall, I feel like I can share Deep Personal Secrets and Ultra Revealing Facts about my life with you now. Like about my mother's hysterectomy.

I could tell you all about my mother's hysterectomy. But the problem here is that she didn't tell me about it either. Not until months after it was all over, anyway. She didn't want me to worry, she said.

So let's talk about something else. Something as big as life and death.

The Difference Between East and West
The difference between East and West is how we deal with life and death.

SLIDE:

DECLINE MAYHEM

(The performer puts on the biggest, silliest fake smile.)
The difference between East and West is:
In the West, we value individuality.
In the East, we value community.

In the West, we value progress.
In the East, we value tradition.

In the West, we value feelings.
In the East, we value subtlety

In the West, life is sacred.
In the East, life is cheap.
(Go ahead, it's a big continent, go ahead, bomb it.)

In the West, death is a terrible thing.
In the East, death is just part of the cycle of life.

I was at a close friend's funeral
and I wasn't feeling too great.
All I wanted to do was sit by myself and cry for a while.
And this white Buddhist comes up to me and says,
Why are you crying?
Don't you know that death is part of this whole cycle.

In the East, mourning and grief is a passage, a necessary rite.
In the West, mourning and grief is a sad thing.

You must be so irrevocably assimilated to be crying like that, he said.

(Starting with something resembling mournful restraint, and crescendoing into a mad sheer-abandoning saliva-spewing rant.)

This Is Not a Hysterical Angst-Filled Performance Art Monologue
And I look down the street
and all I see are men strangling their little children
snuffing the life right out of them,
    I see panhandlers demanding more
as people get more numb to everything around them

Attack of the Man-Eating Lotus Blossoms

I see rapists and muggers and molesters
I see murderers and swindlers and religious zealots
And I want to get numb too

And I look at the hospital
and I see men lying in green hospital smocks
having their insides scraped out
I see women lying in green hospital smocks
having their insides scraped out
And every tumour, ever malignant cell
that creeps into our consciousness:
AIDS, cancer, breast cancer, heart disease, gunshot wound
AIDS, cancer, breast cancer, heart disease, gunshot wound
And I want to be numb numb numb
    numb numb numb
numb numb numb

And then I look around,
and I see my friend Robbie and he's dead;
and I see Frank and he's dead,
and I see Alice and she's dead,
and I see Bob and Daniel and Pam and they're all dead dead dead.

And it seems that no one seems to care.
And it seems that no one seems to notice.
Why not take their dead bodies, smear paint on them, stick them on the wall and sell them as art.

(A double take.)

Oh, wait a minute, that's not me.
That's some Karen Finley monologue I once saw.

Sorry about that, this also just keeps happening.

It's not that a disproportionate number of my friends aren't dead from AIDS or suicides or cancer or something or another, but that's my bag, not yours.

Justin Chin

EXQUISITE VICTIM #1:
(In the manner of a charity infomercial.)
"Hello.

Every year in America, thousands of people die from AIDS. These once-vibrant people, who enriched the lives of so many Americans, are now thin and weak, a shell of their former selves; they suffer all sorts of skin diseases and internal parasites; and they slowly lose the functioning of their liver and kidneys and eyes; some even develop dementia. Oh, it's just horrible.

But there is hope. The AIDS Network Welfare Project Charities is doing all it can to help these poor victims of this horrible disease. And you can help too. For a small donation of $35, we will be able to clothe and feed these poor people and get them the medications and nourishment they need.

For your gift of $35, you will receive a 8X10 glossy photo of your very own AIDS sufferer, a personal handwritten letter of heartfelt thanks, and yearly updates of your own special person's progress. But more than that, you will be putting a smile on one poor AIDS sufferer's face.

If you are able to contribute more, would you please consider donating $50, or even more? Won't you please give now?

If you call now, we'll also send you a free digital sportswatch and this beautiful canvas tote bag. Fifty-dollar donors will also receive a specially requested song at the next AIDS Dance-a-thon, a specially made embossed bikeseat cover at the next AIDS Bike-a-thon, and a pair of inscribed wine glasses at the next American Music Awards Celebrates LIFE benefit fund-raising dinner, dance, and silent auction.

But more than these wonderful and useful gifts, you will be doing your part to help end the suffering of thousands.

Don't do it for the gifts, do it for the thousands and thousands of poor people suffering from this dreaded disease.

Attack of the Man-Eating Lotus Blossoms

Thank you. And Happy Holidays."

SLIDE:

DECLINE NOSTALGIA

Foot Rubbing
You want the true story. I make no guarantees here.

(The performer picks up the lightbulb and holds it in the palm of one hand. The fingers wrap around the bulb so the audience sees bits of light spilling out from between fingers. The bulb will be hot, but who said life was going to be easy?)

Some men would rather go blind, have their brains rot to mush inside their skulls, have rat fungus covering their entire alimentary canal from the tips of their tongue right down to their rectum, than get KS.

On the other hand, there are those who, covered with lesions, spotted like a Dalmatian, are still sitting in the park happily giving blow jobs as they have for the last ten years, living off the semen of the desperate, the closeted, and the horny, the bar dregs, the midnight cruisers.

Matthew is someone I sort of know. When you live in San Francisco for a while, you sort of know people. Friends of friends, people from the neighborhood, favorite-haunt regulars, people you see almost every day of your life whom if you even know their name, you're one step ahead. You greet with a nod, you smile, you see each other in various places.

Matt used to date John, an acquaintance of mine. You have to understand that if there were to be poster children for the gay couple, these two would be it. John was buffed, incredibly good-looking (he even appeared on some greeting card that may be found in the fag card shops). He decorated his little apartment tastefully. He was in social work. He was charming. He wasn't all that bright, but face it, when you're buffed, good-looking, on greeting cards, can decorate, charming, *and* in social work, people stop counting already. And he had a goatee, and really good hair that seemed to move on its own even when there was no wind. People wanted this man, and Matt got him for a while. And even then, Matt was also buffed and good-looking and smart and charming. You get the picture: they were a great-looking couple.

I first met Matt at John's birthday party a few years back. I was one of the many that were so smitten by the two. I would have played happy homewrecker with such ease, but no chance, they liked men who looked like them. It's hard to imagine a community of gay men who look like buffed models who only date each other, but damn, it does exist. It's almost like some gay Nazi genetic-breeding experiment created to breed buffed fags who will live to pose for *Advocate Men* and *Honcho*. (But enough of my neurosis, and back to the story, which again, may or may not be true.)

(The performer picks up a slab of raw meat. Doesn't have to be a good cut, but the wetter, rawer, and bloodier the better. Drape the meat over the lightbulb. If the bulb is hot enough, the meat may sizzle faintly, faint vapors of steam may also show. The performer holds the lightbulb with the meat wrapped around it. If the meat is thin enough, the lighting will take on a rather lovely meaty glow.)

Eventually, they broke up (and not on good terms, I might add), and I still saw Matt around town. At cafes, at clubs, at the gym. (Yes, I went to the gym, believe it or not.) I had been introduced to Matt a few times before, but he never showed any sign that he ever remembered me, ever knew I was alive. Even when he needed to work through my set, he never acknowledged me, never asked me if he could, and all I could do was hang around and hopefully try to sniff him. (There is a point to this whole story.)

But one day, a friend and I were at coffee and we bumped into Matt. We started chatting. Matt had just been through a rough illness and he had started to break out in KS. He insisted on wearing tank tops so that he could scare the sweater queens in the Castro. People who used to cruise him fiercely chose to not make eye contact with him ever since the KS, he said. KS or not, damn, he looked so good in that tank top.

Attack of the Man-Eating Lotus Blossoms

Anyhow, one thing or another happened and we ended up at his place, sprawled on the living-room floor chatting about stuff.

My friend had to leave and Matt and I ended up chatting. It was a pleasant conversation even though he never recognized me ever from anywhere.

(The performer starts to massage the meat, as if it were the aforementioned man's flesh. Be careful of the dripping fluids from the meat; it may seep into the light socket and could possibly electrocute you.)

In his last bout of dementia, Matt had a vision where God (or at least his version of God, he admitted) crawled under the covers and cuddled with him as he tried to sleep. God was kind of tall and skinny, had an average cock, but good low-hanging balls, he said. Matt said that he thought God would have a better body; after all, he is God.

(By this point, it should be clear that the performer is really massaging the meat, and not just playing with it. Really put some force into the act.)

The day was dragging on, evening was setting in, and the conversation was dwindling. He said his feet were hurting. Without any forethought, I took off his boots, took off his socks, and held his left foot in my hands and slowly rubbed it. Massaging the ball of his foot, the heel, gently pulling at his toes, rubbing on the flats of the toes, pushing my fingertips into the groove and arch of his foot. I repeated this on his right foot. There was one spotted lesion on the top of his right foot, and it bled as I pressed into it a little too hard. He leaned back and breathed softly, his eyes half-closed. I massaged his feet for a while. When I finished, I looked up from his feet; I saw that my palms were stained with his blood.

Before I left, we hugged tightly, and he said, That's the closest thing I've had to sex in such a long time.

(Pause. The performer smashes the meat-covered lightbulb. If it's

possible to do with bare hands, do that. Otherwise, use a hammer or better yet, step on the meat-bulb. The collapse of the glass, the fluids in the meat, and the live electrical current will cause a gorgeous pop and spark. Be very careful when performing in a country with a 220V system.)

A Song in My Heart (or, Stars on 45)
I cannot describe how it was I felt:

(The performer hastily picks up the remains of the meat-bulb, cupping them in both hands.

Very seriously, very earnestly, and oh so truthfully.) It was as if someone had left the cake out in the rain. And I didn't think that I could take it, because it took so long to bake it, and I knew I would never have that recipe again.

> [Yes, it's from "MacArthur Park." Okay. Here's the score: due to the prohibitive cost of securing permissions, not to mention the hours of back-breaking hassle, the full text of *A Song in My Heart* as performed cannot be published, regrettably.
>
> *A Song in My Heart* is composed using snatches — one to three lines of lyrics — culled from popular songs, somewhat, if not instantly, recognizable to the average Top 40 radio listener, hence the *Stars on 45* subtitle. The snippets of song are strung together as seamlessly as possible — grammatically, and in terms of sense and syntax.
>
> At the beginning, the piece is performed with huge aplomb, Feeling, and Truth; the choice of songs and of lyrics fuel this Cavalcade of Sentimentality. But as the piece progresses, as song snippet follows song snippet follows yet another, the performer's acted emoting starts to sag, to weary under the heft of this ludicrous language that is not his own.
>
> This is the pivoting point: as the performer succumbs? surrenders? submits? to this language, the only language available for him to use, the tone of the piece changes. Now, the lyrics, and the sentiment invoked in them, are imbibed with a strange gravitas;

Attack of the Man-Eating Lotus Blossoms

there is a strong undercurrent of genuine feeling and emotion. It's even oddly moving.

I suppose one could use any combination of songs and song bits, but the ones I chose were, in order:

- Donna Summer's version of "MacArthur Park"
- Meat Loaf's version of "Paradise by the Dashboard Light"
- Joni Mitchell's version of "Woodstock"
- Joni Mitchell's version of "River"
- Bette Midler's version of "The Rose"
- Tina Turner's version of "What's Love Got to Do with It"
- "I Dreamed a Dream" from the musical *Les Miserables*
- "Don't Cry for Me Argentina" from the musical *Evita*
- Bonnie Tyler's version of "Total Eclipse of the Heart"
- Barbra Streisand's version of "People"
- Janis Joplin's version of "Me and Bobby McGee"
- ABBA's version of "The Winner Takes It All"
- ABBA's version of "Super Trouper"
- "Memory" from the musical *Cats*
- Whitney Houston's version of "Where Do Broken Hearts Go"
- Paula Abdul's version of "Promise of a New Day"
- Melissa Manchester's version of "Don't Cry Out Loud"
- "Send in the Clowns" by anyone who's ever covered it (though I favor the Lou Rawls version)
- And finally, ending with Frank Sinatra's version of "My Way" (though Nina Simone's version works it so much better every which way)]

…without exemption, I planned each careful footstep, alone by the way, much more than that I did it my way.

(The performer lays the meat and glass gently at his feet. And the lights fade out. The next thing the audience sees is:)

Justin Chin

EXQUISITE VICTIM #2:
(The only lighting comes from a string of lightbulbs, maybe eight or nine of them, that is hanging out of the performer's mouth. One of the bulbs is fully inside the performer's mouth, making his cheeks glow, the blood vessels filter the light so that it is reddish orange. The performer/character is also standing precariously on a wooden box. It should look uncertain whether the chain of lightbulbs is being swallowed or vomited.

The following is prerecorded; it is spoken flatly and unemotionally, somewhat mumbled even. There is an odd warbling sound in the background, which comes from a New Age self-healing audio recording being played backward.)

"There are more than 30 million people infected with the AIDS virus in this world. There are 16,000 new infections every day. Every seventeen seconds. Every five-and-a-half seconds. One in every hundred sexually active adults is infected. Only one in ten of those infected know.

5.3 million people were infected in 1996. 5.8 million people were infected in 1997. 2.3 million people will die in 1997, a fifty percent increase over 1996. Half of these people will be women and a half million of them will be children. Only six percent of people with AIDS in the world have access to drugs.

I am HIV-positive. What makes me think I'm anything special?"

(The lightbulbs turn off one by one.)

Do Little
(The performer returns to the pile of meat and bulb. He unwraps the meat and shows it to the audience. There should be pieces of glass embedded into the meat. That's just the way lightbulbs shatter. Hopefully, there will be some big shards. The performer picks out the chunks of glass and places them in his open palm. The hand is slightly outstretched as if the performer is offering the glass shards to the audience, or he could be begging them for some — no one can tell which it is since it could equally be either.)

I came to reading and writing through *Reader's Digest* and Dr. Doolittle books.

Attack of the Man-Eating Lotus Blossoms

My favorite part of *Reader's Digest* was "Drama in Real Life," where there was a literary account of a drama that happened in real life: floods, shopping mall collapse, semi-eaten by carnivores, tornadoes. When a local hotel collapsed without warning in 1985 and made it to the pages of "Drama in Real Life," I was so excited. I read and reread that account over and over, chewing over every detail.

"Animals You Will Never Forget" were the real lives of animals that were humans' best friends. The veterinarian's horse, the WWII pilot's dog who helped him cross enemy lines, the blind girl's cat, the owl in the barn, heroic dogs and loyal cats. The only thing was that each and every animal would die on the last page.

I liked Dr. Doolittle books. I used to hide the library copies behind boring science books so that no one would check them out and I could have access to them. I loved the idea that someone could walk and talk with the animals, laugh and sing and dance with the animals.

The one story that I loved the most was the one where Dr. Doolittle and his entire household meet the Giant Turtle, the oldest living animal in the world. The bulk of the book consisted of the Giant Turtle recounting the Great Deluge to the Doctor. The Great Deluge that God had sent to destroy the earth that had sinned so miserably, sparing but Noah and his family and the male and female of every species of animal. Seven pairs of clean animals, and a pair of unclean animals.

And I remember thinking, the Turtle survived, the fishes survived, the amphibians survived the forty days and forty nights of rain. And I remember thinking, the Bible lied, Sunday School lied, God fucked up. He tried to kill everything, but he fucked up. Some still survived. And discovering that, knowing that, gave me so much hope.

(Not that I have anything necessarily against God, whoever He/She or It is. I would like to offer a prayer as I have been taught to.)

(During the prayer, the performer holds his hand up and outstretched, in full view for audience and God, and slowly clenches it. The performer proceeds to crush the glass pieces in hand, grinding them; the effort shows on his knuckles, which are white with the force

of the action, and in a slight tremble. During the pauses of the speech, the audience can clearly hear the glass cracking and crunching, as the performer unrelentingly keeps on crushing the glass in his hand.

If this is done correctly, the performer's palm [and some fingers] should bleed. Profuse bleeding should always be saved for paying audiences.)

A Prayer
God:

This is prayer and not a rant, as I am wont to do. I am tired of ranting. I am so tired.

Many years ago, when I was a child, I asked my parents, the church elders, and the youth group leaders why, if you existed, there was still so much disease, pain, suffering, war, famine, and car accidents in the world. Why did the cat have to die? I was told to have faith, to believe. Later, I asked what if everything I was told was not true, how could I be sure if you existed? I was told to have faith, to believe.

Now, I am still a child. I want to grow up so much.

I ask for assurance.
I ask for the absence of fear
I ask for the absence of flight
for protection,
for anger when it is right
for calm when it is right
for sense
for reason
for rationality
for articulation
for love
for rage
for will
for quiet
for a decent wage of self-deception
for sex
for awareness

Attack of the Man-Eating Lotus Blossoms

for strength to carry on
for the bother to carry on
for the will to carry on
for desire, whatever that means these days

God. I have been faithful, I believed in my own way.

From backrooms and bathhouses, cruising parks and alleyways, bars and places so encrusted with filth and dirt, from bedsits shooting up with people I hardly know and sharing all-night sessions of booze and tweaking, crashing beyond all levels of this body,

I have been faithful, I believed in my own way.

From surviving bashings with nothing more than a bruised ego and body, from crawling out of accidents with nothing more than nerves. From funeral to funeral to memorial, grief to despair to loss. From bitterness and cynicism, hope to revival,

I have been faithful, I believed in my own way.

The other night, late night I couldn't sleep again, I was watching television, the public service advertisement where a pack of gay bashers armed with baseball bats have cornered a preppy gay man. The bashers spit out epithets, Faggot, Queer, Homo, names I have loved in my life. The gay man pleads with them, *Please, what have I ever done to you?* This is intercut with images of a rabid pit bull. The screen then fades into the message "Hate: It's Not Human." This troubled me, I couldn't sleep. This is not the message I want for my people, your people. I wanted so much for that the preppy gay to pull a gun out of his Brooks Brothers briefcase and shoot everyone of his bashers. And the screen will fade into the message, "Self-Defense: It's Only Human," or "How to Stop Gay-Bashing."

This will never happen. It is only a fantasy, but that's all I seem to have left these days. But for the 987 men and women who died from being bashed last year, they don't even have that anymore. I'm told you have some pull with Death, please visit these people and be good to them as you haven't been in life.

Justin Chin

Here's another fantasy.

A cure. But I live too much in fantasy these days. Some folks says its good to have fantasies, but I'm not sure. It gives me too much hope I think. In the time of this prayer, another 25 people will have died from AIDS around the world, another 157 will have seroconverted. I will know some of these people. Some of these people will know me.

I'm sorry, maybe it's my fault, I'm taking up your time when you should be out there helping these people. But I'm a selfish bastard, you know that, and I want some of your time. Give me tolerance for red ribbons that I see everywhere. For the safe-sex posters that blend into woodwork like stain. For misguided efforts and anger. For vague multicultural Safe Sex posters in eight languages leading to a phone line only staffed by English-speakers. For Safe Sex education that feels it needs to have colored faces simply to stem criticism. For colored folk who demand this, an excuse, you know the argument, I didn't know about Safe Sex because the education was targeted at white gay men only, no one ever said I didn't know I could use Nike shoes because I didn't see myself in the ads. For my homeland, where seroconversion is getting out of hand, and fear and accusation is high, I ask for hope.

Lord, give me denial
if not give me delusion
give me disregard
give me abandon

I want.

Give us back our sense of invincibility,
our ability to love and fuck without fear, guilt, shame, or regret.
If fear, give us five more years of life.
If guilt, give us seven more years of life.
If shame, give us ten more years of life.
If regret, give us twenty more years of life.
To make things right again.
God. I am close to not believing anymore.

Attack of the Man-Eating Lotus Blossoms

Do something.

(The performer opens his hand, showing a bloodied palm and crushed glass; there may be splinters embedded in the palm or fingers. The performer tips his hand toward the ground and lets the glass bits fall from his hand onto the ground. He lightly brushes off the pieces that are stuck and plucks the splinters out. The falling bits of glass fragments finely collide and clash so that it sounds not unlike the tinkling of a child's bedtime toy, heard two rooms down.)

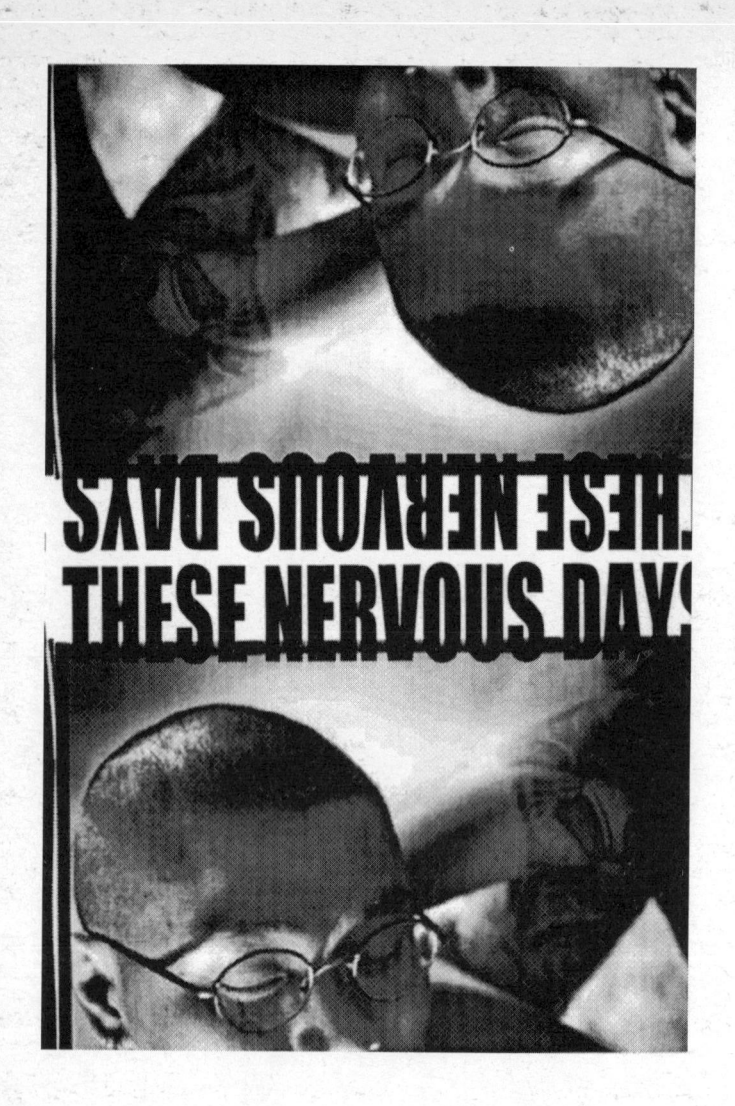

THESE NERVOUS DAYS

These Nervous Days (1995-1999)

While *Holy Spook* is the most performed work, *These Nervous Days* is probably the most known work.

At the time, I was interested in the idea of immunity, not just in its medical sense, but also in its various forms, associations, machinations, and metaphors — political, social, personal, in memory, in storytelling.

These Nervous Days was a difficult one to do, losing a few cups of blood and making a bloody mess notwithstanding.

On a few performance, things were going not badly, but not well either. The performance was at a point where it could go horribly sour and disappoint, or it could salvage itself: that usually meant that I was running out of time, and I could not find a vein, because I was too dehydrated, it was too dark, or the tourniquet wasn't doing its bit. Something.

On a couple of occasions, I decided to tenaciously dig in and go for the vein, pulling the syringe out and resticking it in my arm again and again, trying to draw just a decent amount. Blood would be dribbling down my arm, on my trousers, pooling on the floor, or dripping in sprays and splotches. These shows turned out to be some of the more interesting performances of the work, if not simply for the freak-show masochism involved.

If I remember correctly, only one person ever fainted. A number of people did leave quite in disgust, or bored (and one or two complained). But those who were squeamish mostly chose to look away or look down at their feet, or walk to the back of the performance space and have a quiet sit down.

Shows where I did get a clean draw of blood, where the audience's response was decidedly more engaged and the performance itself turned on a different point, at the final gesture in the piece, were among my favorites. When the carton was opened and the milk first poured out, there was usually a little shock, a bit of a surprise, a small gasp. The color of the milk mixed with blood, and the densities of the fluids involved, produced a liquid that looks familiar, beautiful even as it is simultaneously sickening.

In some versions of the show, there was a video projected on the rear wall. The video showed stuffed animal plush toys being abused and molested, interspersed with distorted (by being played at various wrong speeds and directions) clips of classic Hollywood movie "deathbed" scenes, and extreme close-up frame-by-frame shots of various eyes.

***

(The performer is seated at the head of a long table that is set lengthwise to the audience. There is a small pile of windup toys on the table. The performer unhurriedly winds up each of the toys and sends it shooting, walking, crawling, bobbing, or springing down as much of the length of the table as possible before it falls off the table's edge. On some performances, there is a video projection in the background, consisting of a montage of death scenes from movies — classic Hollywood, action movies, Westerns — played in slow motion.)

Faces of Death. That was the cool movie to have seen in school. Kids whose parents were less strict, and kids whose parents had accounts at the good videotape-rental stores (the ones with the extra, hidden stash of blue tapes and X-rated tapes bundled up in newspaper and passed secretly under the table), had all seen *Faces of Death*. But worse than that, they talked about it; and anyone who hadn't seen *Faces of Death* was so utterly uncool.

What was there not to be fascinated by in *Faces of Death*: man eaten by alligator/crocodile; monkey brains being eaten from a live monkey; girl jumps from sixth floor; scores of Arabs being decapitated; medical autopsies they would never show on *Quincy M.E.*; airline crashes; car crashes; train crashes; bicycle crashes; horse falls on a jockey; satanic cannibal rituals; convict in the electric chair; psycho father slashes family's throats. The latter admittedly did strain the movie's credibility.

When we finally got a videotape player for the house, oh, I

Attack of the Man-Eating Lotus Blossoms

prayed that my folks would bring home *Faces of Death*, but it was *E.T., Poltergeist, Orca: The Killer Whale, Ghostbusters, Jane Eyre, An American Tail, The Deep, Ice Castles*.

Needless to say, I did not see *Faces of Death* until I was well into my twenties.

Faces of Death is a pseudo-documentary, directed by—according to the press materials—Conan Le Cilaire. His bio reads: "A young and dynamic director, Mr. Le Cilaire has directed adventure stories from diving to scalling(sic) mountains. He is a man with a great love of celluloid. The intensity of *Faces of Death* will no doubt place him in a league all his own amongst his associates in the film world."

The main character in *Faces of Death*, your guide, your Virgil, if you wish, your narrator, is Dr. Frances B. Gross. His bio reads: "Not only has he worked as a county coroner, but besides, the Doctor is in the middle of compiling a biography of his experiences of death that he has seen during his lifetime."

Every work of filmic genius needs a writer, and *Faces of Death* is credited to Alan Black. His bio reads: "Mr. Black has been associated with Dr. Gross for the past five years. Aside from assisting the doctor with his forthcoming book, Mr. Black has worked as a 'film doctor' for numerous movies throughout the world. He is a man who has forgone credit on many pictures, because he prides himself as an idea man, the man who can take a weak picture and make it a success. *Faces of Death* is the first feature in which he has granted the use of his name."

In case you haven't seen it, *Faces of Death* is mostly stock and newsreel footage of accidents and wartime atrocities. Most of the footage is badly filmed staged events—superextreme close-ups and bad continuity give it all away, not to mention the bad special effects makeup, and the blood that is just too red. The only real dead people seem to be the bodies in the morgue. And even those seem like an instructional film from some 1950s medical school.

Dr. Gross, the narrator, looks like the Crypt Keeper, and the narration and music is way overblown. Incidentally, in *Faces of Death* 2, Dr. Gross gets a makeover. No longer the shabbily dressed narrator of #1, he's in a leather jacket, knee-length boots, and safari trousers, and rides a motorcycle. In *Worse of Faces of Death*, a compilation of #1, #2, #3, and #4, Dr. Gross dies while undergoing surgery by his colleague Dr. Louie Flellis. I ask you: is this not entertainment at its most entertainingest?

As a kid, the movie held such a curious marvel over me. More so than *Shocking Asia*, *Shocking Asia II*, *True Gore*, or *Death Scenes USA*. Maybe it was because the film promised faces, though it never really delivered.

My parents believed in the educational value of movies. There were always lessons to be learned. Things my folks learned from movies and told me that I should do in the event of calamity:
   1. If a swarm of bees attack you, try to dive into a pond of water. (We had just seen *The Swarm*.)
   2. If there is an earthquake, try to hide under a car. (We had just seen *Earthquake* in Sensurround sound and Steve McQueen.)
   3. If there is a fire in a tall building, try to get to the roof where the helicopter can get you. (We had just seen *The Towering Inferno* starring Steve McQueen, again.)
   4. If the devil or a possessed person is in your presence, protect yourself by invoking the name of Jesus Christ, cite scripture, or say loudly and authoritatively: "In the name of Jesus Christ, I command you to get thee behind me." (*The Exorcist*. *The Changeling*. *The Amityville Horror*.)
   5. Don't swim at night because sharks will eat you. (*Jaws*)

You are born and then you die. I first heard about death from the Bible. Not any Bible, but the *Children's Illustrated Bible*. The *Children's Illustrated Bible* was a huge tome, as hefty as a library dictionary. It was old and musty, the cover was wrapped in a hard plastic wrap, and it had been passed down from older cousins who had outgrown it and moved on to the *Good News Bible* or the *New International Version*. The *Children's Illustrated*

Attack of the Man-Eating Lotus Blossoms

Bible was more of a storybook than a Bible. It would take the good stories from the Bible and retell them in a storybook manner, but with big colorful pictures.

One afternoon, after lunch, my brother and I sat on my grandmother's bed while she read to us from the *Children's Illustrated Bible*. In her room that smelled of 4-7-11 eau de cologne and Prickly Heat powder, she opened the book and read to us from the Book of Revelations. There was a picture of a street showered in balls of fire; the inhabitants of that street, dressed in faux Middle Eastern clothes as only Christians can imagine Middle Easterners wearing, were reacting in horror. It was the end of the world, my grandmother told us, the Second Coming of Christ. And unlike the first time when God destroyed the world by attempting to drown it, this time he would destroy it by fire. "And your daddy and every one who does not believe in God will die," my grandmother told us. This scared the bejesus out of my brother and me. We started bawling our eyes out, and we ran to our mom who told us that we were safe, saved, because we did believe in Jesus Christ as our personal Lord and Savior.

The idea of the Rapture and the Second Coming of Christ stayed with me for a long time. I was enrolled in a Methodist school and even there, once a year, during chapel, the teachers would play some Christian film, which seemed to have been made in the early '70s, about the Second Coming where the faithful would be snatched from the earth and the others would be left to face The Beast and a millennium of evil and godlessness. In the world of Christian media, Rapture films are in themselves a viable genre. I was terrified to be left alone, day or night. In thunderstorms, and every year we were struck with monsoons, whenever I was left alone, I would be terrified that it was the Rapture and I was unprepared.

The *Children's Illustrated Bible* wasn't all fire and brimstone. It also had some cool stories. One of those cool stories was how Moses saved the Israelites from slavery in Egypt. I always thought that the best part was when Moses goes to Pharaoh and, after stalled negotiations, brings the plagues on Egypt. There was the Plague of Blood, where all the water in Egypt turned to blood. The Plague of Frogs, the Plague of Gnats, the Plague of Flies, the Plague of Locusts, where the country was overrun with the mentioned insect pestilence. The Plague of Livestock, where the cattle and fowl mysteriously died. The Plague of Boils, where the Egyptians got horrid skins lesions. The Plague of Hail, where huge balls of the hardest hail rained down for days. The Plague of Darkness, where it was dark. And finally, the mondo-supremo, the big cheese: the Plague of the Firstborn, where the Angel of Death killed all the firstborn in the land except those whose houses' doors had been smudged with goat's blood. "Does it have to be goat's blood? That's so messy," I asked. "Can we not use chicken or beef or iguana's blood?"

"You must obey what God tells you to do," the adults replied.

(By this time, all the windup toys should have been sent on their way.

Also on the table, midway, is a stack of pills and capsules. These must be real pills, or look like real pills, not the fake fat vitamins pills, or the ugly herbal pills. The pills must look very pharmaceutical. The performer proceeds to eat these pills one, or two or three [depending on how many pills there are], at a time. If there's a great mountain of pills, by all means gobble them up like some hungry Third World goat that has stumbled upon the grassy knoll. If the performer can swallow the pills without water, that's great; if not, take small sips of water to help them down.)

I've come to realize that God was actually more practical than not. Take for instance, the resurrection: Jesus was not the first to be resurrected, that trick was first pulled on Lazarus. Think about it: if you're going to pull a resurrection, you really ought to first test it out on someone other than your only begotten son.

And so it was with the plagues on Egypt. God had this whole plague thing/idea/concept, and it needed testing. Who better to use than the Third World, which was then the First World. Apparently, he could have used any of the other developing civilizations, the Euphrates and the Nile weren't the only rivers, you know. But what the heck, the Egyptians were good enough — they were sinners, had lots of money, and

Attack of the Man-Eating Lotus Blossoms

a lot of spare time. The test markets proved successful and the product line went on a real full-speed roll, kicking out new flavors, new models, every so often.

I imagine Plague Central in heaven to have a support center, where helpful volunteers and those working off their purgatory, sit and answer letters written to God regarding plague-related topics, on-line, by post, and on their daily drive-time radio call-in show. "Hi, from the Plague Offices, Paul from Minnesota writes, *I have a series of boils in my ass, could it be some kind of plague*? Well, Paul, let's see? Yup! It's venereal! Our germs and viruses are made from The Best Stuff in Heaven."

In 1000 BC, the Chinese started the first immunization program. In a dynasty wrecked by smallpox, they found a way to inoculate: by picking the scabs off the dead, pounding the bits into a fine powdered snuff, which was forced into the nose of the living. Which only leaves me to wonder just WHO in any frame of mind — sober or perverse or demented — would even have a smidgen of such a disgusting idea as picking a scab off a dead body and eating it?

Immunization programs were big in the newly developing world. In the '60s, Singapore and Malaysia had found their independence from years of colonial rule, then from the Japanese occupation, and one of the main goals was a stringent immunization program to protect the newly independent masses from smallpox, diphtheria, rubella, and a whole host of tropical diseases with Occidental names. At school in Primary Six, we were all herded down to the quadrangle, and made to take a TB skin-blot test. The BCG/TB inoculation was enough to even drive the toughest kids to tears. The test was a small smear of dead TB cells scraped into the crook of the forearm and a week later, it was measured. If the blot was larger or smaller than one centimeter, you were ushered to The Other Line for the dreaded BCG inoculation. For the whole week, we watched the spot in our arm where the needle had pierced. Some kids' blots swelled to a large spot while others almost disappeared. Mine didn't seem to change much and looked like a mosquito bite. Then the dreaded day came and the nurses from the health department showed up in their van, in their starched uniforms and funny nurses' hats, and they set up shop outside the disciplinary master's office. Wilson Lim had the fabulous last-minute idea of using his steel ruler to enlarge his pinhead-sized skin blot. He scraped away but got it too big and was dragged away in tears, screaming all the way up the line where he was jabbed. The BCG injection was huge. The needle looked like a javelin. The shoulder where it was jabbed would swell for a week and it hurt like nothing any of us had experienced before. It was hell. All week, we would sneak up to other kids and punch them on their swelled arm. A lot of tears were shed in those weeks. Worse than that, the spot where we were inoculated would turn crusty and the spot would fester and scab horribly. My brother had the good fortune of knocking his shoulder into the side of the school bus. His scabby crusty spot bled like mad but then his crusty scab fell out and he does not have a scar, any mark to show for that injection. I on the other hand have two scars on my right arm. The girls were shot in their hip, thereby not marring their arms and spoiling their chances at supermodel stardom or the chance at a good dowry.

I toughed out my inoculations without crying. I had to. My father was a doctor and I would accompany my parents to work at the clinic. Mom worked the dispensary. Actually, I had to go with them as there really wasn't anyone who could be bothered or had the time to babysit me in the evenings. So I became one of the many Chinese kids who accompanied his parents to work, sitting in the back, reading my school books, and being generally well-behaved so my parents' patients could admire how well-bred I was, or how much I'd grown since the last time they saw me. It seemed that most of them last saw me when I was two feet tall.

It's a funny thing having your dad as a doctor. I never could get a doctor's note to skip school. Dad would just pump me full of drugs and send me off to the school bus. My school chums all seemed to be able to skip school like mad. But the real pisser was that they also managed to skip PE with silly excuses like swollen ankles, hormone deficiencies, and, the mother of them all, The Ear Infection, which was good for at least six weeks. Yolanda, Elaine, and Renee seemed to have their periods every other week. Later, I learned how to forge a sick note and school started to be a bit more tolerable.

Attack of the Man-Eating Lotus Blossoms

The other right downer was that I had to take all my medications and injections without flinching. My brother had a lot of trouble swallowing pills. He would gag and have this silly look on his face, then water and strange semidiluted pill bubbles would form at the sides of his mouth. I did not have any trouble swallowing pills. I felt that my parents should have loved me more because I could swallow pills and he couldn't. When it came to injections, my dad would have none of the screaming and crying of "No, nooooo... I dooooon't waaaant, wahhh," that he had to put up with from other little feverish children brought to him. My brother and I had to tough it, hold out our arms, look away, and take that sharp pierce of needle and the burning flow of medicine into our veins. My dad gave me my Hepatitis-B booster shot at dinner. He finished his meal early, disappeared to the kitchen, and returned to the dining room with a loaded syringe. He firmly tilted me thirty degrees over, pulled down my pajama trousers on one asscheek, and stuck me at the dinner table while I was still holding my chopsticks over my bowl of chicken flat-noodle soup.

There is a certain level of equivalence at work here that is untold. My learning to stand stoic-arm or -buttock out before my dad's injections being equal to his learning how to jab us. When I was born, Dad was still working at the state hospital to pay off his scholarships and loans. We're told that Dad was never able to give us our inoculations. He always had to get his colleagues to do it and he could never watch. He would wait outside the room, leaving Mom who was a nurse there, to hold us. Later, after opening his own clinic, living in the back of it for years, he finally toughened up and was able to jab his own sons. Perhaps we weren't the lovable little tots we once were, perhaps Dad just got used to the act, sticking injections in too many patients.

The balmiest thing about having a father as a doctor is that I have ended up placing an inordinate amount of belief in the assumption that if I ever got sick, Dad would make it all better — science and medicine were on his side. Hence, I have developed such blind faith in hospitals. The antiseptic smell, the urgent rush of nurses, the display of medical paraphernalia and technology lying carelessly in the hallways like toys in a messy apartment; it all reassures me.

Justin Chin

(Also on the table is a metal kidney dish, the kind used in operating rooms. There is a syringe in it. While continuing to talk to the audience, the performer uses the syringe to draw as much blood as possible from the crook of his arm, or any vein that is convenient. This might take some time. But if the task is finished quickly, the performer holds the syringe daintily in hand between thumb and third finger, like a joint, or an offering.)

Before I left for America, I decided for various reasons to take an HIV test. For obvious reasons, I couldn't go to Dad. This meant that I had to call up the Ministry of Health to get an appointment. I called, got the appointment. Which meant I had to go to the Communicable Diseases Center, which coincidentally was only two blocks away from our family church. So here I am sitting with hookers and housewives whose cheating husbands brought home more than chow hor-fun for supper. I'm sitting with sheepish men whose hands cover their crotch as if their bony carpals would ward off the antibiotic-resistant gonorrhea. The sexual-disease folks face one way, the TB people face the other, the chairs are arranged this way; the government doesn't want us to bond in the shame of our communicable diseases. The walls were once white, the building was an old colonial mansion, but now it's where one goes to get sores scraped out of one's genitals. (Which might all make such a delicious comment on colonialism if anyone would stop scratching their balls, dabbing pus leaking from flaming urethras, and calming nerves to even consider it.) Any moment, you expect a leper ringing a bell to come through, but the only bell is the loud clang followed by CHIN, AIDS TEST, ROOM 23. Everyone turns to look at me as I stand and cross to room 23; syphilitic cows, gonorrheal slags, and folks who don't even have lungs anymore stare at me as if I were the leper with the damn bell, well, *ring my bell baby, ring-a-ling-a-ling...*. The doctor was a middle-aged man, he opens his log. There are sheets of names and he goes through the list, asking for statistical information. Are you gay? he asks. I say NO. He checks off YES. I peep at his sheet and apparently he had marked off ARE YOU GAY? — YES for everyone. He pulls out another list and starts reading it to me, the usual stuff they tell you at any health department. He's telling me all this, but I'm focusing on the view outside of the window behind him. There

Attack of the Man-Eating Lotus Blossoms

is a hooker across the street, leaning out of her shophouse window trying to sun her rather enormous black brassiere. I "uh-huh" periodically and he is satisfied. I am sent to another room where this nurse, who may or may not have worked for the Japanese Gestapo during the Occupation of 1941-1945, is sent to take my blood sample. She sticks the needle in and draws the test tube full, pulls the needle out, and gives me a ball of cotton the size of an old lady's molar. The blood doesn't seem to want to clot and there's a small stream of blood flowing down my arm. After all, the needle and equipment seems to have been saved from her Gestapo days. Can I have another gauze or cotton ball? I ask her, but Gestapo Queen says that she doesn't have anymore, go down the hall and ask at the desk. Down the hall means I have to walk in front of the same syphilitic cows and gonorrheal slags to get a damn cotton ball. Which at this point I have no choice, and so I dash across the hall to the station with my arm still streaming with blood. The nurse looks up bewildered and to stop me approaching her any more than necessary starts tossing cotton balls across the table at me. *Fuck it all*, and I go across the street to the local chemists to buy a box of Band-Aids, never once looking back.

The sense of taste is closely related to the sense of smell. If you can't smell something, you can't taste it. This easy fact was quite useful when it came to gulping down the government-issued milk that I was forced to drink during my year in Primary 2. The lumpy lukewarm milk mixture, bused in by the Department of Education, was actually meant for children whom the teachers suspected were malnourished. But since the suspected malnourished children were far too busy playing catch or chatek during recess to bother about the government's efforts at fattening them up, the canteen lady in charge of ladling the lumpy gruel, needing to get rid of the supply, decided to simply force it down anyone who came by, even obese little me.

When you ingest poison, the medics will tell you to drink milk because it will retard the absorption of the poison. We used to believe in the goodness of milk.

The morning glass of milk was a hand-me-down tradition,

Justin Chin

passed down from one generation fearful that their pork-fat children would starve to another fearful generation. For my mother, it always began with the Indian man pushing his dirty Raleigh up the back lane, back wheels rustling in the lallang, up to our rusty back gate. Grandma would fetch her purse hidden under the sofa cushions, or in the piano seat, and go out to meet the man to get the latest gossip from his side of town — who's beating who, who's sleeping with who, who eloped with who, who said what about who, who died — and to get two bottles. Fresh, milk fresh this morning, he swore. Milk from two anemic goats chained to the tap under his mango tree.

Grandma knows goat's milk. Goat's milk must always be boiled first to kill the germs. Goat tits are quite dirty, apparently. To get the full value of the milk, Grandma cracked three eggs into the simmering milk, stirring while the slimy transparent white disappeared in the steam, the yolks burst and colored the milk a yellow tinge.

For a time, we had to drink goat's milk too. We didn't really have a choice, not with Grandma's bamboo cane (50¢ at the market). We would rush to the kitchen to be the first in line to choose the mug with the least milk. (The one with the blue bird on it until some dumb cousin broke it.)

When she was little, my mother tells me, Grandma made her drink that damn goat's milk too. Mom would take three sips and pour the rest down the drain. Three sips so she wouldn't be found guilty in Methodist Guilt Court and sent straight to hell where demons cut your tongue out for saying, "I drank my milk," when really you poured it down the sink, or worse than that, being caned on the tongue for lying. Mom was caught, of course, by Grandma who was hiding behind the fridge. Grandma was suspicious Mom always finished her milk first. Mom was sentenced to drink double portions for two weeks while watched by the cane. It's nutritious, Grandma said, swearing by goat's milk as a preventive measure for I forget which eight major ailments.

For us, we progressed from goat udders to the wonder of Nestlé powdered full-cream milk. One heaping tablespoon, one tablespoon of MILO to taste, maybe some condensed milk and hot water.

No one ever suspected that I was seriously lactose intol-

Attack of the Man-Eating Lotus Blossoms

erant. There it was every morning: the dreaded glass of milk on the kitchen table. It took less than a minute before a skin formed on the surface of the drink. But my elders had this fear that I—us, the children—would somehow die of malnutrition, so I was forced to drink the milk. I would hold my nose and chug it down in as fast a gulp, in one motion, as fast as possible. Then I would board the school bus, belly sloshing with milk, and at the end of the forty-minute journey I would get off the bus and vomit. Later, I would learn to control the ralphing and just shit it all out in a glorious squishy pile.

This I did for years.

Once I was forced to see a psychiatrist. I hated him immensely. I made up stories. I looked him straight in the eye and told him that I always felt that there was something crawling about under my skin. General paranoid stuff so that he'd prescribe good drugs for me to resell to get better drugs. He asked me about my relationship with my mother. I told him that my mother substituted her nipple for Nestlé. He nodded knowingly and started scribbling excitedly in his pad. Later he came up with this really great theory that my sexual deviance and my lactose intolerance were due to my low self-esteem. Play more sports, he said.

According to some Chinese superstitions, illness can be caused by the disharmony of elements and energies in your body. The spiritual see it as a battle between the forces of good and evil in the body. A more medical view looks at it as a huge battle on a microscopic level.

In kindergarten, during art session, I once created a series of crayon drawings depicting the life of Humpty Dumpty. Even at that tender age, I was such a conceptualist. I was not a great artist and Humpty was easy to draw. The series portrayed the Egg family in their daily life and in their partaking of earthly pleasures: having a picnic at a waterfall, going camping. The one that amazed my kindergarten teachers, and got my picture on the wall, was this picture of Humpty Dumpty and his egg pal (the details of their relationship are not important). They lived underground much like earthworms, but were undoubtedly real eggs, eggs which could be scrambled at any moment.

The two characters were in their underground room where they shared a microscope. Humpty Dumpty was looking into the microscope and the cross section–enlarged cutaway showed what he was viewing: a slide of bacteria, germs, and viruses in all the colors of the crayon box.

(Also on the table is a small carton of milk. Try to use the 250 ml pack, or the smallest sized one you can find. During the next bit, the performer takes the syringe and slowly but firmly plunges it into the top of the carton. Holding the carton up to eye level, the performer slowly pushes on the syringe's piston. When the carton of milk is fully injected with all the blood, the performer very slowly pulls the entire syringe out and holds the empty bloodstained syringe as previously held.)

It is not a coincidence.

Pollen never used to be in the news. Every year, the pollen count gets higher and higher, and allergy sufferers suffer and gobble more designer antihistamines and pray at the altar of snot and phlegm for some relief, but the oracles are grouchy.

Every year, scientists and doctors discover more germs and bacteria and viruses that are more resistant to anything pharmaceuticals can come up with. But the pharmaceuticals keep trying, whipping together a concoction, blessed with FDA approval, Madison Avenue imaging, and it is a new sacrament, a new host for our penitent lips.

Every year, new pests, new insects, old pests, old insects walk right through our new and improved Raid, Roach Traps, Ridsect and take a vengeful shit in our food.

Perhaps it's some karmic payback for when we bought all those lantern bug-killers, thinking that somehow little flying bugs would be attracted to a frequency or luminosity, but the only bugs that got fried where the ones who were going to fly through it anyway, the ones we stuffed into it, and those that needed light to navigate: moths and beetles, poor buggers. It's like Rand McNally on some homicidal binge.

Every year, I find more friends getting some kind of cancer. I find more friends in their twenties being diagnosed as manic depressive and their doctors dishing out antidepressants like M&Ms. I find more friends seroconverting. I find friends' young children developing strange food allergies. I find new

Attack of the Man-Eating Lotus Blossoms

unheard of opportunistic infections lurking around the corner. I find myself wondering when was the last time I had a good clean breath.

It is not a coincidence.
   We are becoming less immune and we are at a point in our culture where we are at the point of evolution. Happens every so often, every couple of millennia, every day, and here we are, lucky us, smack in the middle of the naturalest selection, suspecting that we'll need new bodies to cope with the chaos.

It is not a coincidence
   How people are incorporating iron into their lives. Armoring themselves with guns and bullets, piercing themselves in more places, suiting up for a slosh through cyber-whatever. Some search for new skin, remapping their bodies in new ways. Some crave new bodies, bending their genders to follow their hearts' desire. Others are found praying for GNC's promises of Nirvana. Pray for the Miracle of Our Lady of Jenny Craig. Some try to live beyond their bodies, midnight raving with Dionne Warwick and her psychic friends, who will give TRUTH at $3.99 a minute, fifteen-minute minimums, an optical fiber smart-drug of epiphanies that *anybody? anybody!* can partake of. Bless me, holy mother of Visa and Amex.
   Some try to find safety by hating and condemning. Witness the rise in fascism, in immigrant-bashing, in hate crimes that so many governments won't count, in closing borders and deporting difference. Witness the Great Dancehall of the Politically Correct, with five lanes to justify any vile hatred and petite disdain, and in the next room, the xenophobic tango is in full swing, babes.
   Some try to incorporate into another culture. Asian homeboys rapping their ways into the REMs of the American Dream; for so many young Asian kids these days, it's more important, cool, normal for them to want to be black rather than Asian. White Hindus overrunning Calcutta looking for the answer and a good bargain in Indiany stuff. Hey, if you can't afford the Sex Tour of the Third World, join the Peace Corps.

Justin Chin

All these words, hysteria, paranoia, theoreticizing, and dread.
All these nervous days.
It is not a coincidence.
As we inch toward the millennium, we wonder,
what do we use to gain admittance to a new world of less pain?

(Following the instructions on the side, open the carton of milk, and pour the milk out into a glass. Use a clear glass. If done correctly, and the lighting is favorable, the milk is stained a brilliant and gorgeous muted pink.)

Everything has been swept away.

I see a history called lifetime.
    I see a lifetime burning down.
        I see the death of the body.
            I see the death of the nation.
    I see the death of the family.
        I see the death of memory.
            I see the death of nostalgia.
                I see the death of borders.
                    I see the death of the sky.

            I create my culture everyday.
        I write a bible of diaspora.
    I bruise in broken speech.

And what are you gonna do?

            I say I will find a new place that is mine.
        I say I will find some place
I say, I say,

I say.

(Lactose intolerance aside, the performer drinks the bloodstained milk in one continuous gulp. If it's in any way possible, try to have a milk mustache or small dribbles of milk running down the chin.)

TAKE A HELLRIDE FLASHBACK TRIP TO SOUTH EAST ASIA OF THE 80'S

fringe: BORN

a performance by JUSTIN CHIN

"Just the raw stuff of serious risk-taking."
--San Francisco Bay Times

"It's always worth seeing what he comes up with next"
--On-Q Bay Area Magazine

"A tremendously talented and inspired writer"
--San Francisco Sentinel

"...no holds barred... He's a master at the world's most over-used instrument, the voice, making it by turns seep like melted government margarine or spit like a kitten on speed."
--San Francisco Bay Guardian

"His subject matter is written with sensitivity; eloquent without being overbearing. He's definitely going places. Make sure you see him so you can brag about it later when he gets really famous"
--LA Weekly

SURF REALITY, 172 ALLEN ST.
SUNDAY 8/17 8 p.m.
MONDAY 8/18 4 p.m.
TUESDAY 8/19 10 p.m.
WEDNESDAY 8/20 5:45 p.m.
FRIDAY 8/22 8 p.m.
SUNDAY 8/24 noon

ELEVEN DOLLARS
for tix: 1.888.374.6436
for info: 212.420-8877

Born (1995-1998)

It seemed that everyone had put aside the novel or the play they were working on, and was working on a solo show. At that point in time, you couldn't toss a paperclip down a sewer and not hit someone who had a solo show in the works. Solo artists and actors performing their monologues were all over the city. Heck, it was nationwide. Monologists were scoring Off-Broadway and Broadway deals, HBO offers, movies roles, gushing write-ups in the papers and magazines, and all the love an ego could coddle.

In a silly way, I felt pressured to create something more narrative, more audience-friendly. Compounding this urge were the inquiries, for a spell there, of a number of curators and art programmers who kept asking if I was thinking of doing something more narrative, something more conventional in form and structure, something that they could sell to a general audience.
    And so, I started *Born*.
    The piece didn't quite fulfill the threat of the narrative arc, though it did lean in that direction.

With *Born*, I was trying to work all the unreliable biography out of my system. Looking at it now, I see that the piece has a strange voice. It's either a serious voice about fake things, or a fake voice about serious things. But all that is way too serious in any case. And if you get from the work some ideas about narrativity, its constructs, and unreliable storytelling, then you're thinking way too much. If anything, *Born* was meant to be good, silly, fun, and entertaining.

***

Dance to the Music
With the help of hypnotherapy, psychotherapy, art therapy, and aromatherapy, I'm coming to terms with that short period in my life when I took breakdancing lessons.

Justin Chin

When breakdancing exploded onto the scene, no one expected that it would only last one paltry year. Especially not after the smash hit movies *Breakin'*, *Beat Street*, and *Breakin' 2: Electric Boogaloo*. No one expected that breakdancing, with the pops and waves and various back-, neck-, head-, and wrist-spins, and elaborate legwork would disappear faster than a spider on speed, certainly not all the recording artists who used breakdance motifs in their videos. The oh-so-hip "Let's Hear It for the Boy" and "I Feel for You" now look so dated, but then, then they were objects of celluloid nirvana, to be scrutinized, replayed at slow forward, and analyzed to unlock their secrets of that spin, that twist.

No one predicted the end of breakdancing. Certainly not the Rocksteady Crew, whose "(Hey You) The Rocksteady Crew" went all the way to #4 on the Singapore Broadcasting Corporation Radio 1 charts. Certainly not Break Machine and all the other nameless bands that catered to the headbanded masses eager to pop, wave, and backspin.

Certainly not Lim Seng Chin who broke his right wrist and left arm while demonstrating the wristspin-backspin combination. Certainly not Alvin Tan who broke his neck while attempting the perilous headspin in the period between Advanced Mathematics and Chemistry. Certainly not the hundreds of kids who ended up in hospital emergency rooms and intensive-care units after they snapped, broke, and sprained miscellaneous limbs and joints and caused the government to declare a nationwide crisis on juvenile delinquency, but still these kids wore their casts, slings, and neck braces as medals of honor.

I took breakdancing lessons from Ibrahim Saleh, who two years earlier had won the National Disco Dancing Champion-ships. He was trying to diversify his portfolio. I was one of those kids who couldn't figure it out by myself and I was too embarrassed to ask my friends. Locking myself in my room, which was a misnomer because the rooms in our house didn't have locks, I dusted the floor with Johnson's Baby Powder and proceeded to practice, but I never got any good or anywhere. Maybe a semidecent wave, a little pop that looked like a muscle spasm, and one and a half, maybe two, backspins that looked like a terrier scratching its back on a tarmac dusted with talcum

Attack of the Man-Eating Lotus Blossoms

powder. But even after that measly backspin, I was always too confused to know how to get into the correct pose. The talcum powder wreaked havoc on my allergies and my tender sinuses and forced me to give up practicing all together.

The process of dancing has always eluded me. I am not a good dancer. I cannot dance when I'm sober. I probably still can't dance when I'm sloshed or cranked, but then I don't care, so it's all right. I'm one of those '80s kids, when dancing was a completely different thing altogether. I never really figured it out and till today, I still dance like one of the extras at the new wave club at the beginning of *The Hunger*. I project this image of myself, and I think that I'm so cool, not unlike one of the dancers on those pointless dance-party-type television shows, but then I suddenly catch a reflection of myself in a club mirror and I just scare myself at every turn.

My first introduction to dancing was at the 1980 Prinsep Street Presbyterian Church camp. After lights out, Gillian Fok, the richest girl in church, taught us how to do The Hustle. Since no music was allowed, except really catchy hymns and praises, we took turns softly singing "Night Fever" while we learned from a tattered instruction book smuggled into camp, titled *Disco Fever*. It proclaimed, YOU CAN DO IT (2 Exclamation Points). The book was whipped out and we learned in the dead secret of a church camp night.

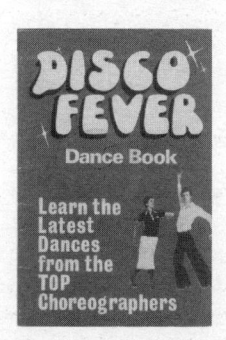

You can see how I was destined to failure.

Justin Chin

From disco to high energy to house to techno, what a way to go. I learned to dance in the '80s at a function that a girl from another school threw at her daddy's country club. She was a friend of a friend and I got invited. It was my first function—coolness in school was calibrated by the number of functions one got invited to and actually did go to. Helen Lee grabbed me and asked me to dance. I sheepishly said I didn't really know how, and she cheerily said, "It's easy, I'll teach you! Just move your feet to the beat!" But it wasn't like *Dirty Dancing* where Helen's sense of rhythm and love of movement inspired me to Nureyevian greatness. Instead, it was Helen trying not to look like an idiot, constantly snapping at me, "You're not moving *with* the beat! Listen to the beat!" But it was hardly my fault, the extended remix of "Party All the Time" isn't exactly the most booty-inspiring song, if you know what I mean.

It wasn't that I didn't have the dance in me. George Clinton once said "Free your mind and your ass will follow." I knew it was somewhere in there and it could be lured out. Oh give me Martha and The Vandellas, Smokey and The Miracles, Marvin and Tammi, the Supremes preaching "Baby Love" and I'll shake it on down, twist and shout, do the mash potato, the twist, travel to the land of 10,000 dances.

I did not dance in public for another year. Then I met *him*. He wanted to meet at The Niche and I panicked.

The first gay disco I ever went into was called The Niche. It was on the top floor of Far East Plaza, a local shopping mall. Clubs and discos in the Singaporean '80s were always found in malls and shopping centers. Everybody knew about The Niche. It was always said in the same breath with a nervous laugh, with something self-deprecating, something protective added, all a full octave lower. People knew people who saw someone go to The Niche, but no one ever saw anyone themselves.

The Niche was on the fifth floor of Far East Plaza, on the far corner just down the corridor from Crest, the mega Christian bookstore. The Niche was dark, with blacklight (Oh My God! How Cool!) and neon. It had a smallish dance floor with squared panels of primary-colored plastic and a lounge section that overlooked the dance floor. My first taste of The Niche proved addicting. I downed a screwdriver and danced, remembering what Helen Lee had tried to teach me about mov-

Attack of the Man-Eating Lotus Blossoms

ing to the beat. Maybe the faggotty dance music was easier to move to. Maybe it was the place, maybe it was the motivation.

Pump up the volume, when the drumbeats go like this, the song ordered and I danced. A year later, Legends opened. Another gay disco, this place was better. It was better lit, had more space, and the ambience was much better than The Niche. Overnight, The Niche became the sleazier hole-in-the-wall place where the evil trolls gathered, while Legends became the trendy place. (I miss the days when gay bars had names like Secrets, Phazes, Traxx....)

I can't survive, can't stay alive, the high-pitched falsetto voice thrilled over the thumping speakers and we danced. We dance over heartbreak and heartache, over boyfriends who ran off to Thailand every month, over unerringly straight boys we were in love with, over the fear of being found out, over that closet door creaking open, over failing grades, over the strange sense of the rest of our lives hopelessly settling in our guts.

We danced, and when we stopped dancing, we looked up, our bodies were sweating, our limbs and hips were tired, we looked up and we saw that the world had changed before our eyes.

I don't know for sure because I didn't see it in the papers but my friend told me about it one night at Legends. A German tourist at the Holiday Inn had AIDS and was deported immediately. The room was sprayed with disinfectant and all the furniture was burned by government officials in asbestos suits. He said he saw the officers in their space suits dash across the lobby. I wanted to know more, but the DJ started playing "I Wanna Dance with Somebody (Who Loves Me)," Whitney Houston offering her message of romantic idealism, and he just had to dance.

I Wanna Dance with Somebody Who Loves Me. Now that's an interesting idea, isn't it? Not marry, not suck, not blow, not fuck, not diddle, not buy Crock-Pots with, not kiss, not have lunch, just dance. What a tease.

It makes me think of the run of guys in my life.
And so, a deviation: Here is...

Justin Chin

88 Lines About 44 Boys
(The performer holds up at arm's length a small tinny tape deck that plays the song "88 Lines About 44 Girls." The following is performed to that song, over it.)

Randy was a Christian boy, he held out but for not too long.
Steven was a different type, he's the one who swallowed all.
Sammy was a fat boy, and I sometimes liked a boy like that.
Alex painted pictures sitting down in the toilet stall.

Marvin was an aimless fuck, a geographic memory.
Peter was a New Age freak, he liked that kind of misery.
Alan had a special way of turning sex into a chore.
Homer Fong couldn't fuck, beat his dick, beat it raw.

Richard was an archetype, the muscle queen, the queen of duh.
Tom thought men were second best when masturbating in the tub.
Erik was an anarchist, he really had that gift of gab.
Gordon's point of view was this, touch whatever you can grab.

Roberto was another boy who left his mark upon the bed.
Rodney liked to tie me up and spanked me lying on his lap.
Kenny had this awkward walk, walked like a stick was up his ass.
Billy-Ray who had a wart said it would go but never did.

Frederick the last taboo was shattered by his balls one night.
Charlie brought the taboo back and held it up for his ass.
Theodore who knew no shame was never ever satisfied.
Johnny came and came so fast, I didn't even get his name.

Marty had a house in Maui lived on brown rice and poppers.
Terry had a house in Oakland ate cough syrup by the case.
Donald thought his life was pretty, filled it up with alcohol.
Kenneth was too much too dippy, the older trolls paid for his car.

Eddie thought that love was simple, stick it on and pull it off.
Anthony was complicated like some French filmmaker's plot.
Russell was the perfect man, always kept his lube pristine.

Attack of the Man-Eating Lotus Blossoms

Walter was a masochist, pierced his dick with rusty nails.

Norman was a modern dancer, butt so tight and bouncing right.
Franky wrote bad poetry and made me read it every night.
Robert, bearish, like to fuck while wearing leather biker boots.
Gilbert's strange obsession was for certain vegetables and fruit.

Fenton was an activist, protesting all his day and night.
Roger's brother left his lover, took his dildo and his bike.
Benjamin had no such problems, perfect Beaver Cleaver home.
Victor, sixteen, had bad zits, lunar craters in his moons.

Macon joined the PETA band and annoyed his friends to no end.
Danilo who played guitar sang songs about tits and cocks.
Eugene didn't give a shit, was stoned and passed out fifty days.
Irving was so much more messed up, he wrote songs about cheese.

Gregory went forty days drinking nothing but martinis.
Michael drove his Chevrolet into the San Francisco Bay.
Philip came from Ohio, he's a Scientologist.
Dashell, darling, here's a kiss, I chose you to end this list.

88 lines about 44 boys.

Hey, Turn That Thing Up
Every time I have to go through a traumatic time, I cocoon back into my teenage years spent lying in front of the radio: I fancied myself a teenage existentialist poet, clad in black (well, Day-Glo was that epoch's black; I was well within my rights), rebelling against the norms of genteel Chinese society. And I really liked to listen to Casey Kasem's Top 40 countdown. So many reasons to like this broadcast standard. But mine were: 1.) I didn't have that much money and I wanted to tape some stuff off the radio; 2.) We lived near a swamp and that was the best radio signal after the twenty-four-hour Koran station; 3.) Casey Kasem is the closest you can get to postmodern gothic terror on FM-radio.

Justin Chin

There is nothing better than lying in bed on a monsoon evening listening to Casey Kasem's countdown:

"Mary-Ann Wilson from Bumfuck, California writes:
Dear Casey, I had a brother who I loved very much. When we were kids, we used to hang out and play, we weren't just brother and sister, we were best friends. But one summer day, I accidentally backed the station wagon into him and broke his leg in fourteen places and cracked his hip into three. He would never make the U.S. Olympic Judo team that he had been training fifteen years for. I know I shouldn't have driven the car, after all, I was only thirteen. To make a long story short, Casey, when he was in the hospital, his girlfriend ran off and married her ex-boyfriend, who was the recruitment leader of a militant spiritual cult. My brother was depressed but not as depressed as his gangrenous legs and then we discovered that he also had cancer and soon after, the shingles set in. My mother started drinking and my father got arrested for possession and distribution of child pornography, the cat gained weight and died of a heart attack, and the dog got hit by a pickup truck when it tried to run after a rat. My whole world was falling apart, but Tim helped me pull through from his ultra-germ-free intensive-care oxygen-tent bubble. Casey, my brother died last year after being in a coma for ten years, and I just wanted to dedicate this song to him to tell him that I miss him and I'm sorry for all the wrongs I've caused him. Tim, if you're out there listening, this song is from your sister Mary-Ann. She wants you to know that she loves you and misses you.

"This song is also #4 on this week's Top 40 countdown, that song is Wham!, with "Wake Me Up Before You Go-Go."

Casey Kasem's Top 40 and the other request/dedication shows showed me something, that no matter what problem you had, what trauma you were going through, what sort of pain you were experiencing, there was a song for it.
Break up with your boy-/girlfriend? "Saving All My Love for You" by Whitney Houston. Miss your divorced parent or estranged sibling? "Somewhere Out There" by James Ingram and Linda Ronstadt. Want to chase that grand dream? "Fame" by Irene Cara. Regret? "Hard to Say I'm Sorry" by Chicago.

Attack of the Man-Eating Lotus Blossoms

Need encouragement during manual labor? "When the Going Gets Tough, the Tough Get Going" by Billy Ocean. Cat run over by a car? "Total Eclipse of the Heart" by Bonnie Tyler. The pain of kidney stones? "I'm Still Standing" by Elton John. Herpes blisters hurt? "Up Where We Belong" by Joe Cocker and Jennifer Warnes.

In 1984, I bought a cheap pirated $2 copy of Prince's *Purple Rain*. The album cover featured a paisley border of violets and carnations and Prince, lit in purple, sitting on his purple motorbike in a purple brocade suit, his Jheri-curled splendor framing his heavy eye makeup and that Prince pout; in the corner was Appollonia in a purple frock; and everything on that album cover was being threatened by a massive purple fog. Alerted by my brother, my mother got worried and called me in for a quiet chat. Actually, it wasn't quite a quiet chat. She screamed, "What kind of music is this! Is this satanic?"

Satanic music was a *big* concern. Bootleg tapes of a lecture by American evangelist Jerry Anderson were widely circulated in school, and on the tape, Rev. Anderson explained the evils of pop music. The Rev. Anderson talked about how record companies would hold satanic black masses to bless a record before a release, how sex, drugs, and booze were rampant and perverse but deemed to be normal. The Rev. Anderson showed us how album covers hid secret satanic symbols, like the pentagram, the ankh, the inverted cross, and the little lightning flashes that are found in the typeface of AC/DC and Kiss. These lighting flashes just screamed SATAN.

(Here, the performer randomly pulls out a stack of record covers from a larger box of covers and sleeves. He meticulously points out all the hidden symbols and all the subtle codes, as well as the glaringly overt ones too, on these albums that point to satanism. Olivia Newton-John's may prove to be difficult some times, but none quite as difficult as Gloria Estefan and her Miami Sound Machine's. Their winks to Satan are frightfully subtle. But it's there....)

Most chillingly, it talked about Backward Masking. For those less familiar with the world of Satan and his Evil-ettes, Backward Masking is the satanic science of placing secret hymns, odes, and Hallmark greetings to Satan in a backward code in the grooves of records. These messages would subconsciously infect the virgin ears of good Christians, and the undecided, and turn them into sexual-deviant pot-smoking animal-sacrificing Lucifer worshippers.

I took to backward masking with a vigor. I wanted to find out for myself, but the road to truth wasn't easy. Sure, the Rev. Anderson gave examples, but who really gave a flying fuck about Styx, Black Sabbath, Blue Öyster Cult, and Black Oak Arkansas. I wanted to know about the music I was listening to. Was Morrissey the pawn of Satan? Did Depeche Mode kill goats so that "People Are People" would break the American charts? How did Phil Collins ever get so popular without the help of the darkest powers? Could anyone explain any part of Sheena Easton without visions of hell? I was determined to uncover this secret code for myself. It was long hard work but one night, I struck paydirt. Men At Work's "Who Can It Be Now?," already a suspect lyric unmasked, read "All I Need Is Satan." Which meant that "Down Under" might not have been about Australia after all.

Then the shock: Cyndi Lauper on "Girls Just Want to Have Fun," revealed her true satanic intent. But why take my word for it, let's just hear Cyndi worshipping Lucifer herself, shall we?

(The performer holds out another dinky toy cassette tape player. When the tape recording of "Girls..." is played backward, the chorus will actually yield the nasal chanting of "Oh Satan" repeatedly. Spooky, isn't it?)

Oh Satan. There, we have it. Cyndi worshipping Lucifer All Through the Night, Time After Time. While Feeding Sally's Pigeons. That's What She Thinks, (when she thinks about you).

It fell like dominoes: Michael Jackson's "Beat It," Sheena Easton's "For Your Eyes Only." It seemed like that one night I had peeked into the gates of Hell and I had to play my grandmother's hymnal tape to exorcise the tape deck and to quell the heebie-jeebies I had raised.

All this should have made me give up popular music, but then, like breakdancing, the backward masking paranoia faded out, leading to the accompanying *E.T.* conspiracy where we

Attack of the Man-Eating Lotus Blossoms

saw that the similarities between *E.T.* and Jesus Christ, our Lord and Savior and Messiah, were frighteningly similar. That Steven Spielberg was trying to set up the spongy foam-rubber alien with the voice of Debra Winger as the next messiah. But that soon faded out too and things churned on as always.

My interest in pop music started early. Influenced by my cousin Leslie, who was the same age as I was, we were big ABBA fans. Leslie's sisters, Hazel and Mabel, were air stewardesses, so he was just the most cosmopolitan person I knew. Hazel and Mabel Chua weren't just air stewardesses, they were air stewardesses for Saudi Air. When aunts talked about Hazel and Mabel, their lips would say the girls were air stewardesses but their eyes said, Fallen Whores of Babylon. Leslie Chua and I sat in the school bus with our ABBA tapes and had arguments about who we wanted more to be: the down-to-earth but golden-voiced Frida, or Agnetha, voted sexiest bottom in all of Europe. The *Voulez-Vous* album was incredible for Benny and Bjorn's innovative use of orchestration, especially on "Kisses of Fire." But the next album, *Super Trouper*, was the best thing ever created by a living human being. It has taken me thirteen years, but I have finally understood the heartbreak and pain of that album. You cannot understand *Super Trouper* until you have lived. The lyrics detailing the band members' breakups and failed marriages with each other is still so raw even to this day, and it's all wrapped in these lovely melodies. My heart breaks every time I listen to that album.

From ABBA, I moved to Boney M, then to Blondie (great leap, huh) and then *Solid Gold* opened a whole new world to me. Yes, *Solid Gold*. This was a time when Dionne still was just a nasal whine with flared nostrils, before her psychic friends would lie to her and say that her last album, *Friends Can Be Lovers*, would be a big big hit; this was a time of innocence and The Pointer Sisters, even way before they dared to jump for your love.

Solid Gold offered a world of endless possibilities, its bright message gleaming in a hazy fog of uncertainty: the music has magic, and I know you can catch it when the rhythm takes control. Dionne gave way to Rick Dees to Andy Gibb and then after Victoria Principal broke poor Andy's heart and sent him into a narcotic depression (and death), Marilyn McCoo took over, singing her one cover song a week. (Her particular rendition of Diana Ross' "Muscles" was disturbing.) It was gorgeous; it was entertainment at its highest and purest form. The accolades and awards do not lie. Eight Emmys (for lighting) DO NOT LIE. *Solid Gold* also offered me the *Solid Gold* dancers, fleshy male dancers in sequins and Darlene, the black braided-haired dancer whose principal choreography consisted of doing leg splits from one *Solid Gold* canister to the next, accompanied by "I've Been Waiting for a Girl like You." (I thought traversing the stage in leg splits was the Holy Grail of modern dance.) Every episode of *Solid Gold* (and to a lesser extent *Kids from Fame*) showed me how much I should be *(failed attempt at an Andy Gibb falsetto) dancin', dancin', yeah....*

But the time I was fourteen, I was deeply hooked into this pop music thing. Every other week, I faithfully bought *Smash Hits* and *No. 1*. Teenybopper magazines with mind-fluffing articles about nothing. They reprinted lyrics which were essential, and they had pictures of videos I would never ever see. In 1984, the band wars were in full throttle. Duran Duran, Frankie Goes to Hollywood, Spandau Ballet, Wham!, and Culture Club were all bitter enemies and so were their fans. We took to defacing the posters and stickers of our pet hates that our classmates had tacked on their file folders and textbooks. I was a Frankie Goes to Hollywood person myself.

As a homo-teen, I had, with a mix of pride and guilt, been big fans of Frankie Goes to Hollywood, Culture Club, and Bronski Beat, who were big buzzes, storming the charts every few months with new singles and videos. I joined the Frankie fan club; I masturbated to my poster of Paul Rutherford. My favorite picture being the one of him in his underwear, the hamster in his boxer shorts was clearly evident, his pierced nipples excited me so. Then I thought that every boyfriend would have to measure up to Paul Rutherford, I'm sorry to say.

I was so into the whole damn scene that I even read the dance charts. And hence one day I discovered this little trashy disco singer called Madonna. She had blazed across the dance charts with "Burning Up" and "Physical Attraction," and now she was going to be on *Solid Gold*. I called all my friends and told

Attack of the Man-Eating Lotus Blossoms

them to tune in. Monday night ten o'clock and Madonna led the show off, prancing around with the *Solid Gold* dancers, singing "Holiday." It was incredible. The next day at school, no one had tuned in to witness this; I was horrified at how idiotic my friends were! I started doing the Madonna look, bracelets up to midforearm, netted shirts layered one on top of the other, funky belts, and shoes. A year later, *Like a Virgin* was released. I dashed to the store to get my copy, I tried to buy a wedding dress, and the rest as they say is history. Soon everyone had Madonna, but I like to remember when she was mine, when I plugged my Madonna tape into my Walkman and crammed for my biology test. (I failed, of course.) And when I showed my fleshy navel for all to see, my parents started to worry that I was displaying not terribly heterosexual tendencies. They blamed Leslie's influence.

That same year, Culture Club had burst onto the scene and the catchy "Karma Chameleon" was everywhere you looked. The previous year's release of *Kissing to Be Clever* was thrilling me; here was a transvestite made good! Up until then, all we ever knew of transvestites was that they all ended up in Bugis Street with crumpled-up newspaper for tits. His genderbender pal Marilyn had also scored a chart hit around Christmas with "Calling Your Name." People said Marilyn made Boy George look like Clint Eastwood. I was a big Boy George fan, as big as anyone growing up in Singapore could be since the government banned the effeminate image of George from the TV screens, afraid that he would entice impressionable youngsters to a life of cross-dressing and newspaper tits. I watched *Solid Gold* and any TV program that showed music videos to see small glimpses of Boy George, who was reedited in Culture Club videos to a bare minimum, a mere background flicker. I wanted to pluck my eyebrows to match his, but my brother informed my mother, who in turn told me that they would never ever grow back and even if they did, the hairs would be bushy and unruly just like pubes, and I chickened out.

December 1984. Best remembered as the "Do They Know It's Christmas" Christmastime. It was during this dizzying "Wake Me Up Before You Go-Go" time when Gloria Gaynor's cover of "I Am What I Am" broke the British Top 20 charts. It was the year when Hi-NRG, with its dinky canned accelerated electro-beats, infused practically everything from Dead or Alive to Divine. Which is a bad example because that's DE to DI, but you know what I mean. Paul Burnett, the DJ that introduced the British Top 20 Countdown on the BBC World Service, said there was nothing like hearing a whole disco singing along with the song. Then again, he said that about Baltimora's "Tarzan Boy" and Sinitta's "So Macho." You got the sense that tenor-voiced Paul Burnett spent a considerable amount of time at the disco waiting for group activities.

I myself liked the catchy thumping beat, the dramatic nature of the song as Gloria whispered the first stanza only to give way to an over-the-top high-energy double-time hand-clapping finish. It wasn't until a month later, when I was sitting at home blasting the song, which I had taped off the radio, that I suddenly realized what it meant. As a gay teenager, I was thrilled yet a tad scared with a bold affirmation of self-identity; I started playing the tape only on my Walkman.

After that, I suddenly realized what all those Bronski Beat and The Communards songs really meant. Suddenly, these lyrics took on a clandestine state of being; I started finding a hidden message of homosexual acceptance and angst in every lyric; it was as if Rev. Jerry Andersdon was happening all over again.

You have to understand. My homosexual longings developed the strongest in the same year as my confirmation and baptism, a fabulous très dramatic immersion baptism. So I was wracked with a lot of guilt and the better part of the year was spent making deals with God, praying for forgiveness and being obsessed with raging hormones and a seemingly endless supply of dicks. I believed that it was all a part of a test by God to see if I was sinning. (I was.) I believed I was destined to Hell. I believed in the Rapture, in the Book of Revelations, a story that had been read to me when I was a mere child and ever since, thunderstorms would cause my heart to collapse. Good Christ-fearing folk would be snatched up from the earth and the rest of the sinners would be left to fight the end of the millennium against the Antichrist. I feared God and the end of the world, but I also feared not having the comfort I found in men.

I feared the distance of knowing and realization. This was

Attack of the Man-Eating Lotus Blossoms

a time of possibilities and of discoveries. Everything was bright and uncharted, and unspoiled. There was no ransom to be paid, no song unsung, no wine untasted.

It was my generation that paved the way for rock concerts in Singapore. After the David Bowie Serious Moonlight Tour, the government was reticent to allow any more concerts that could conceivably promote juvenile delinquency. But then they decided to allow the Gloria Estefan and Miami Sound Machine concert and the ensuing police violence that occurred brought great and profound changes. Bones where broken, arms snapped into piece as batons rained down on the kids who wanted to stand on their seats and gyrate to the Conga. "Come on shake you body baby, do the conga, no you can't control yourself any longer," Gloria implored from the stage in her fire-red hot pants and cha-cha heels. The kids took this rallying cry to be free, and try to be free they did in the face of police batons and threats. And when the government inquiry was over, (the cops had the bad fortune of bashing a minister's son), new rules had been drawn up, and these days, Singapore is a major pit stop and cash cow.

There is an old disco stomper titled "Last Night a DJ Saved My Life." A small tape deck and a mess of tapes did indeed save my life. I learned a language of recovery, I learned a language of my heart and my guts. It may not have been the most articulate language nor the most eloquent, but hell it was mine, it was fine and it slowly learned to be articulate. When things got too much to bear, when the kicks of teenage angst bit hard, when I couldn't conjure up a vision of myself in the future, I filled that space with the soundtrack to my life that I had so painfully pieced together one song at a time.

Another deviation: to acknowledge the process of Coming Out.

An Ode to Coming Out (For Gays and Lesbians around the World America)
(Performed using a bullhorn and volume turned on as loud as possible.)

Justin Chin

We are everywhere.
We are your sons and daughters.
We are your brothers and sisters.
We are your friends and co-workers.
We are your teachers and doctors.
We are your lawyers and lawmakers.
We are your FBI agents and police officers.
We are your architects and designers.
We are your waiters and hairdressers.
We are your convenience-store and video-store clerks.
We are your professors and lecturers.
We are your laundrymen and washerwomen.
We are your veterinarians.
We are your dog groomers.
We are your butchers and greengrocers.
We are your mother's best friend's cousin.
We are your mother's best friend's cousin's daughter-in-law.
We are your cousin's nephew's niece.
We are your nephew's stepfather's brother.
We are your brother's mistress' sister.
We are your grandmother's cousin's adopted son's daughter.
We are the guy in front of you at the express checkout cash-only line at Safeway with a full cart and an ATM card.
We are part of those people who pick all the good meaty bits out of the buffet at Vegas buffets.
We are part of those people that do not pick up after their dogs.
We are part of those people who talk to you on the bus and tell you our political viewpoints whether you give a shit or not.
We are your humorless environmentalists.
We are your politicians and elected officials.
We are your Democrats and Republicans
We are your wacky Third Party candidates.
We are your favorite TV stars.
We are your pornographers.
We are your computer technicians.
We are your *Solid Gold* dancers.
We are your schizophrenics.
We are your manic depressives.
We are your right-wing extremists.
We are your conspiracy theorists.

Attack of the Man-Eating Lotus Blossoms

We are your murderers.
We are your gun-nuts.
We are your serial killers.
We are your Nazis and KKK members.
We are your White Aryan Resistance soldiers.
We are your child molesters and scoutmasters.
We are your priests and your fundamentalists.
We are your friends.
We are everywhere.
Please don't hate us.
Hate isn't human.

Wearing

I saw some younger kids walking down the street the other day and I just want to go right up to them, grab them and shake them and yell, "I wore Day-Glo so that you can have your trousers hanging off your ass. You owe me!"

Kids these days are so lucky that they never had to live through Day-Glo. I always wondered how gay men in the '70s cruised in those '70s bell-bottomed polyester clothes which weren't the retro cool chic we know of it today. But then I realized I was cruising in my Day-Glo outfits. I was a traffic cone with pheromones.

Oh, and when we needed to color our hair, did we have Manic Panic vegetable-dye punky hair coloring? Of course not; we had colored shit in a spray can. (Fluorescent, of course) The dye made you go blind and your scalp smart, especially when it reacted to the industrial hair gel we bought in aluminum tubes. But *dang*! it was so cool. Then. Over-the-counter hairdressing technology has come such a long way.

Someone recently commented that kids these days don't try to look like their pop idols. Then again, even if they did try, it's not like anyone would notice. Pop stars in the '90s just look so normal. It's hardly a challenge. The '80s, now that was a time to model your looks after your pop idols. Your hair's defi-ance of gravity was proportional to the awe you inspired and the cool you oozed.

I went through my Madonna circa "Lucky Star" phase, with netted shirts, funky belts, and arms full of trinkly bracelets. But she changed and I couldn't keep up. So I settled with a Dave Gahan of Depeche Mode flattop that I kept in pristine shape. This was occasionally supplemented with a Gary Numan circa Berserker meets Dead or Alive look. Eye shadow for lipstick (I favored the tanned colors), pale skin, hair greased to *Exxon Valdez* proportions. No one would sit beside me on the bus. My mom refused to allow me to pierce my ears so I cut up curtain rail rings and used them as earrings.

Fashion Victimization is the mother of tacky ideas that seem unbelievably brilliant, begetting cringe-worthy old photos and a shattered self-confidence.

Fueled by the recent Miss Universe Pageant held in Singapore, beauty-queen fever raged. Local shopping malls held beauty contests every other week. Miss Serangoon Shopping Center, Miss Jewelry Mart, Miss Rochor Shopping Center, Miss Electronic Outlet, Miss Wong Nam Wing Sweetmeats and Import-Export Factory.

For the boys, there were look-alike contests. Enter as Prince or Michael Jackson. In any shopping mall, you would encounter all these Michael Jackson and Prince look-alikes. But this was the tropics, and we were all Asian. It was as if the DNA of Michael or Prince were sent to Horrid Cloning Experiment Camp where nothing goes right. It was straight out of the colorized modern version of *The Twilight Zone* which had a short run of only two seasons. Not much creeped or terrorized anymore.

You know you're growing older when you realize there is a generation of kids pushing up from behind you that will not know the same things as you. There will be a generation that will never know how Laura Branigan went from "Gloria," to "Solitaire," to "Self Control," and how we went with her; how she desired street credibility and so released the *Miami Vice*-inspired *Spanish Eddie*. (As if everything from bidets to wart cream wasn't already *Miami Vice* inspired.) They will never know the proper response to "Who ya gonna call!" (For the younger ones, the proper response here is "Ghostbusters!" Go ask an uncle to explain it to you.) They will never know the rapturous pleasure of Olivia Newton-John's "Physical," and how the good girl had gone sexy-bad in her one-hour TV special, swimming with dolphins in splashy phallic splendor. They will never have a knowledge of Melissa Manchester at the

Attack of the Man-Eating Lotus Blossoms

Olympics singing "You Should Hear How She Talks About You" for absolutely no reason. And unless they remake *Ice Castles* with Scott Hamilton and Kristi Yamaguchi, that too will soon be lost. A generation not knowing that Garfield was actually once funny or the terrifying sick fanaticism of *E.T.*-mania in all its anticynical dazzle. Everything in my generation will soon become, or has already become, retro, campy, nostalgic, dated, sad, lost, bought, re-sold. And I would be the moron first in line too.

A Flickering
The Information Age rolled in, a tsunami of choices and gadgets. Certain movies have a way of defining a generation, a cultural epoch: *The Godfather*, *The Deer Hunter*, *Apocalypse Now*, *Taxi Driver*. Certain generations had *Gone with the Wind*, *Citizen Kane*, *Love Story*, or *The Graduate*. I had *Flashdance*. When everyone was rushing to see *E.T.* for the fortieth time, I saw *Flashdance* twenty-eight times. This broke my previous record of watching *Grease* eighteen times.

In that year of raging *E.T.*-mania, I couldn't see why anyone really cared that much about a rubberish little alien who wasn't even cute. No, I much preferred the grimy world of a welder by day, dancer by night who only wants to audition for a shot into the big leagues, the mainstream; and in the movie's case, to dance with the ballet. Totally untrained, she learns her craft from tasteful lingerie dance shows (unlike the ones down at the Zanzibar) and from the street.

I cut the seam out of the collar of my shirts, pulled my sweaters out of shape to get that *Flashdance* off-the-shoulder look.

There was something about *Flashdance* that appealed to me. The idea of making it despite the odds, the idea of liberation and freedom, of transcending the rigid boundaries of class. That, in fact, life is nothing but an audition to get into a place where all the odds are stacked against you.

I had not yet recognized the motif and how it would be redone until it bled. The great thing about being a teenager is that when you discover the wheel, fire, elephants, and existentialism for the first time, you cannot believe that no one else knew about them. Nostalgia works kind of in the same way, but laterally, or maybe in reverse. And in second gear.

Justin Chin

With bells.

For those of you who may have missed this cultural gem, this milestone, our Stonehenge as Flashfans refer to it, allow me now to present *Flashdance*. The five-minute version.

(On a television set or projected onto the screen or wall, the movie Flashdance *starts playing. But seconds past the title, the movie starts to speed up; the whole movie should play in three to five minutes. At the same time, with the same pacing as onscreen, the performer narrates mondo benshi-style the entire movie, with ad-libs and personal observations and comments chucked in.)*

What the '80s Meant to Me
The '80s were much bigger than its popular culture, bigger than pop music and happythings. There was so much more happening, the world was changing, decisions were being made that were going to affect how I and my friends and family were going to live. But what did my tender hinges know of all that? And so like mallrats walking deafly, hypnotized by the Muzak, I walked right into the trap of leisure, the opiate of my senses and my heart. I traded my pickled brains for consumer choice, became the grateful lab rat of The Grand Plan that was gunning toward the greater social blah.

I don't know at what point it happened. It was as if I was waking from a dream of naïve intentions. I opened my eyes and I saw that things could never be the same.

You grow into your heart and your understanding of its past. And you wonder where it has been all this time.

This time period is more than the wink of nostalgia or the serious dash of memory. Of course, I have been selective; I have weeded and pruned and clung to the good bits. I've edited the timeline, crumpled the chronology, merged events, left many things out, exaggerated, lied; I've made things up and I saw things I never saw. I have not told the full story, or a true one. There is no full or true.
    I used to believe that a story was only as good as its intentions. And what do intentions count for in these so little days.

Attack of the Man-Eating Lotus Blossoms

Give me my sense of romance. Give me my revisionism. Give me my nostalgia.

Everything of my queer life, I discovered when things were still mine to hold. Everything discovered, when innocence meant not knowing regret; it was a hot fuck, and AIDS, which showed up so late in that part of the world, was something that was still a rumor. Freddie Mercury was still alive. Rock Hudson had just kissed Linda Evans. The full brunt of the heartlessness was waiting around the corner like the most patient mugger.

These days, I see people I used to hang out with, skip school with; the ones who aren't dead or burnt out, are working their little dead-end jobs, living for the weekend so they can get leglessly spun. People I used to see at ACT UP and Queer Nation meetings, the ones who aren't dead, are working at the designer outlet store, having their little software jobs, clawing onto boards of directors, running for political office, positions we once scorned. We've all grown up so fast, though no faster than any other thing in the world.

My mother always said to me, "Enjoy your youth, you're only young once, you'll never have it again. One day, you'll find that you're too old for so many things. Now stop wasting your time and go study."

I used to know so much, and then I grew up.
I used to believe, and then I grew up.
I used to hope, and then I grew up.
I used to be so beautiful and angry, and then I knew better.

Finals
I would like us — together, collectively, communally — to invoke that different time. And we do that with a song, a very special song that meant so much to so many.

She was a mere cheerleader, a choreographer, but she captured the hearts of the world with a song so simple in its poignancy and its heartfelt lyrics; its innovative use of the budding video medium that added layers of new meaning to the song; its simple yet catchy melody and beat that hearkened back to our primitive sense of being; the sentiments it evoked reached across borders and languages and cultures; it recalled lost youth, lost innocence, a changing world, and it gave us hope. This song touched so many hearts and souls in a time when touching that many people was deemed perverse and dirty and liable to get you locked up.

Yes, I'm talking about Toni Basil. And the song... "Mickey."

(Here, the performer and the audience karaoke along to Toni Basil's "Mickey." Seriously.)

Born
There are two versions of how I was born. One version has my mom in the hospital, an easy birth. The other version has my mom in the back seat of a car in Mersing, a small fishing town eighty miles from my hometown. The birth certificate favors the former. My stunted height, possibly from the lead in car exhaust fumes, favors the latter.

One hundred and eighteen days before I was born, the country had experienced the worst race riots in its history: the May 13 riots had Chinese and Malays in a newly independent nation killing each other with knives, guns, and machetes on the streets.

Forty-five days later, seventy-three days before I was born, in a land far away, in New York, the Stonewall riots happened.

Nineteen days later, fifty-four days before I was born, the Apollo 11 space mission was launched.

Two days later, fifty-two days before I was born, Mary Jo Kopechne died at Chappaquiddick, trapped in a car and abandoned to her watery death.

Two days later, fifty days before I was born, the first people landed on the moon and walked on it.

Nineteen days later, thirty-one days before I was born, Charles Manson and family had committed the Tate/LaBianca murders.

Seven days later, twenty-four days before I was born, Woodstock, three days of peace and music, happened.

And in that three weeks and three days, I took in all the maddening oxygen I could, took in the final formation of skin

Attack of the Man-Eating Lotus Blossoms

and organs, the final swoosh of nutrients, swimming in blood, the kick, the jerk, the curled fetus stretches; the umbilical born, little heart, fist clenched, toes pigeoned in, eyes clenched tight, soft skull, mouth gill-like breathing in strange fluid.

Then I opened my eyes and I was born.

The Asian Art Museum
and the San Francisco Museum
of Modern Art Present

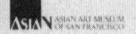

Advice for Tragic Queens at Home and Abroad

by Justin Chin

**Blurred Boundaries:
Beyond the Wall**
*Continuing the performance art series
in conjunction with the exhibition*
Inside Out: New Chinese Art

Sunday, March 14, 1999
2:00 PM

Trustees' Auditorium
Asian Art Museum

CULTURAL PROGRAMS DEPARTMENT ASIAN ART MUSEUM

ASIAN ART MUSEUM
OF SAN FRANCISCO

Justin Chin

Advice for Tragic Queens at Home & Abroad (1999-2001)

And finally.

So, I made it through ten years of performing without getting naked once onstage; the closest I ever got was in *Go-Go GO!* Not that I had any high-minded convictions about it; rather, I just have your standard body issues.

I love the work in *Advice*.... And that's probably all I have to say about it. I think the writing and the conceptual ideas behind the performance of it worked well, or at least to my total satisfaction. *Advice...* also finds me moving away from text-based work. It contains a lot of nontextual pieces, or the text assumes a different form than what I usually have it as.

I swiped the watermelon seppuku bit in *Butterfly* from Stacey Makishi. It's just too brilliant for me to have thought of on my own.

***

Monkey

(The performer enters. Each article of clothing that he's wearing is emblazoned with a stars-and-stripes red-white-and-blue motif, most noticeably his Lycra bike shorts. He has an obscene lump in the crotch of the bike shorts. He puts his hands into his shorts and pulls out a stuffed plush monkey.
He sets the monkey down and carefully removes the pins that are in the monkey's head. Then he carefully peels away the pieces of fabric over the monkey's head. He then holds up a finger and plunges it into the monkey's exposed head, wriggles it around and pulls out a lumpy pasty substance. [Mashed potatoes seem to work best.] The performer calmly uses his finger to scoop and eat the goo out of the stuffed monkey's cranium.)

Justin Chin

Stop All That Insanity

(Performed in the manner of an infomercial or Learning Annex seminar.)

Have you ever fallen in love? Of course you have, and nothing beats the wonderful feeling of being in love. But nothing lasts forever, not even love.

And everyone who has fallen in love has also had their heart broken into so many pieces.

Just when it seems that you have met Mr. or Ms. Right, and it all seems so mutual, then suddenly he or she is "emotionally unavailable" or "loves you but is not in love with you." How many of you have been through a breakup? That is so sad. But I want you right now to know, that it's not your fault, it's his/her therapist's fault.

But with this new program, you will learn how to stop all that insanity that comes with a broken heart.

To begin, you will need to know the difference between a felony and a misdemeanor.

Let's take this example. *(Holds up a toy motorcycle.)* Say your ex-lover has a motorcycle or a motor vehicle. Remember all those fun-filled hours, zipping around from one romantic destination to another, wasn't that a great time? Now, if you should burn your ex-lover's motorcycle or motor vehicle, *(lights a match and sets fire to the toy motorcycle)* that is a felony. On the other hand, if you should smear it with packets of KFC butter, *(extinguishes the flames, rips open several packets of said butter and globs it on the toy motorcycle)* that is a misdemeanor.

Don't ask me why this is so. It's just how the laws are set up to oppress marginalized people.

All right. Now that that is clear, we can proceed.

To get through your breakup, you'll need to follow the few simple exercises in this seminar. It's easy. There are no messes, no hard-to-fill cups, and no expensive nonrecyclable materials. And you can do it in thirty minutes or less and you'll feel so

Attack of the Man-Eating Lotus Blossoms

much better.

Let's have another example. Here, all characters in this example are without exception fictitious, and any similarities to persons living or dead are purely coincidental.

Imagine this scenario:
(The performer uses two plush toys — preferably those with their paws clutching a heart for dear life, you know what I mean — to illustrate the scene.) Let's say you have this boyfriend. Let's call him Lawrence. You're dating, seeing each other for a month, and one day he tells you he's going to L.A. for the weekend to visit an old friend he hasn't seen for a while. That's fine...but then, on Monday morning, you suddenly wake up and realize that he's gone to L.A. to see someone else. You confront him with this ghastly realization, he admits that he did indeed go to L.A. to see someone he met a week ago; they had sex but he reassures you they "didn't fuck." You get pissed off, you quarrel, you try to make up, and then one weekend he says he needs to "take some time away from you," and he disappears to L.A. to finish the fucking. He comes back and tells you that the person in L.A., let's just call the Anonymous Slut, Peter, gives him "what he needs" and that he's the kind of guy that has to concentrate on one person at a time. (Of course, why this rule doesn't apply to you is never made clear.)
    It's a common scenario, right? What do you do?

First, we start with **Creative Visualization**.
    Imagine Lawrence and Peter the Anonymous Slut really getting it on. They're lovey-dovey, dashing through daisy-strewn fields, giggling like little butterflies flitting from poppy to poppy, drunk with happiness in their beautiful, fulfilling relationship while Mariah Carey's greatest hits play from the cosmic ghettoblaster heard only in their love-satiated minds.
    Imagine Lawrence packing up and moving to L.A., because that's where people like that go.
    Imagine them pushing their huge queen-sized marital futon to the bay window so they can look out on the stars as they lie in bed holding hands before they go to sleep.
    "Oh look, honey, it's Astrea Ursa Borealis Major! And there! A shooting star! Quick make a wish! I wish we're

together forever and forever! Oh honey, I wished the same thing too!"

Imagine it's 6 a.m., they're sleeping in each other's arms, and there's a big earthquake. The plate-glass window shatters inward and they're a nice romantic bloody blob which firefighters discover only two weeks later since neither of them shows up for step-aerobics.

I don't know about you but my chakras are really warm now. My aura is simply glowing. For those of you who are psychic, you can see this so clearly. But since most of you are not psychic, it'll look something like this. *(The performer pulls out a flashlight with a green gel taped over the bulb and waves it around his head halo-like.)*

The **Second Step of Healing** is to take some time out to take care of your ex-lover's well-being.

Reading is a good way to help take one's mind off one's troubles. And magazines offer a good range of whimsy.

(Holds up a stack of blow-in magazine subscription cards.) Perhaps your ex-lover would appreciate having sixty or seventy magazines sent to him, billed in three easy installments. Magazine discounters make this so easy, and such a wide range to choose from. He can pick from such exciting magazines such as *Home Improvement Weekly*, *Sesame Street Puzzles*, *Motor Trend*, and *Needlework Digest*.

(Holds up a stack of compact-disc club subscription cards.) Perhaps while reading he would also enjoy listening to any one of thirteen free CDs. Music is always such a beautiful gift. I don't know about you, but I always feel so relaxed and calm after listening to Enya (every time I hear Enya, I feel like I'm on a big fluffy cloud floating over Eastern Europe); or Celine Dion's *Let's Talk About Love*, featuring "My Heart Will Go On."

(Holds up a stack of Book of the Month Club and assorted book club subscription cards.) If your ex-lover wants something more substantial, how about *4 Books for 4 Bucks*. Choose the biggest volumes that he would not normally get for himself. It's not a problem if he's not home to receive all these huge oversized parcels, as the U.S. Postal Service will gladly leave a yellow slip to tell him, "Hey, you got a wonderful surprise waiting for you down at your new Post Office!"

Attack of the Man-Eating Lotus Blossoms

(*Holds up the escort and masseur ads from the newspaper; some of the ads have been circled in red ink.*) Is your ex-lover doing okay with the breakup? Has he shut himself away? Not having a healthy sex-life? You can help. Instead of calling him and hanging up, hoping that he doesn't *69 you or has caller ID, you can look after his well-being by going to the back of your local gay newsweekly, and looking for models who advertise with a pager number. These are trained professionals who can help your ex-lover. And, I'm sure your ex will appreciate getting to talk to a whole host of interesting, good-looking, and well-physiqued individuals. Who knows, maybe he/she will make new friends and these new friends will help him/her get over you.

(*Holds up the page in the Yellow Pages.*) Maybe your ex-lover is the more intellectual or spiritual sort. Why not invite various cult evangelists, Jehovah's Witnesses, Scientologists, and Moonies to come talk to him/her? Just let your fingers do the walking! In the Yellow Pages under CHURCHES or RELIGIONS, you'll find a list of organizations that will call or come over to his house to provide hours of scintillating discussions, gentle comfort, and a good listening ear.

It is only by giving and helping that we can really help ourselves. Remember, breaking up is a vicious cycle, a horrible chain. But we can deal with this, we can break the cycle of breakups, snap those chains that bind us, we can **Stop All That Insanity!** Thank you.

Mea Culpa

(*Stripped down to a T-shirt and underwear, the performer gets someone from the audience to come up onstage, and instructs the person to whip him with a nasty pervy-looking leather whip. Alternatively, a bamboo cane can also be used.*
While being whipped, the performer confesses:)

I'm sorry.

In the third grade, I cheated on a spelling exam. I'm sorry, but in a certain way, I'm still paying for it with bad spelling. But I really am sorry.

When I was six, I killed the goldfish by pouring Singer sewing oil into the fish tank. I'm sorry.

That one thing I said about a certain gay Asian group in a local newsweekly. I'm sorry.

I'm sorry that I laughed when I said that I wouldn't.

I'm sorry that I made fun of all those white Buddhists, I mean, they were just trying to make the world a better place for themselves, and I was being mean. I'm sorry.

That time that I fucked around with my friend's boyfriend. I'm sorry.

I'm sorry for not believing when I should have.

I'm sorry for writing that article about the Mr. Asian of Northern California Pageant; I should have been so much more positive about it. I'm sorry.

But I still stand by what I did write, so I'm sorry to the newspaper I wrote it for, I'm sorry I'm apologizing. I'm sorry.

I'm sorry for being so cynical.

I'm sorry for being sarcastic.

I'm sorry for being selfish.

To my parents, I'm sorry I failed your expectations. I know I could have worked harder. I'm sorry.

To my exes, I'm sorry to both of you. I'm so sorry I failed to be a better partner. I'm so sorry for driving you away. I'm sorry for not agreeing to couples counseling.

I'm sorry I'm not being more grateful for all that I have.

Attack of the Man-Eating Lotus Blossoms

I'm sorry for not being discreet.

I'm sorry for saying I would call and we'd get together and do something when I had no intention of calling ever. I'm so sorry.

I'm sorry that I had unsafe sex that one time. Well, it wasn't once. Maybe it was twice or three times or maybe six or maybe repeatedly. Well, he didn't ask and I didn't tell and I'm sorry.

I'm sorry I'm not a better person, a more decent person.

I'm sorry for taking those tax deductions. They were really stretching in their definitions. I know, I'm sorry.

I contributed to a friend's assisted suicide. I gave him my stash of sleeping pills, and I regret it now. I'm so sorry.

I'm sorry for my tone of voice.

All the times I've questioned anyone's motives, I'm sorry.

To my community, I'm sorry.

I'm sorry I've brought so much shame on my race.

I'm sorry I scratched your car when I was trying to get into that tight space.

I'm sorry for not caring; for not caring more; for not caring some. I'm sorry for not caring enough; for not caring at all. I'm sorry.

I'm sorry this whole thing is beginning to sound like an Alanis Morisette song.

I just want to say that I'm sorry for all the things I have done wrong, all the things I am doing wrong, and all the things I will do wrong.

I'm truly truly sorry.

Justin Chin

Go-Go GO!

(There are three elements to Go-Go GO!*: a text "narrative" on slides, a recorded voice-over narrative, and the performer in character [of sorts]. The entire piece is prerecorded. The performer is in a frightful thong with a social security number pinned to it. The performer/ character gyrates and undulates as only go-go boys in the Third World, with their mystical sexual prowesses and rice diets, can. The slide narrative is projected behind the performer. All of this is played out accompanied by the voice-over narrative, which is recorded over the grooving strains of Cher's "Believe." [Though Techno-tronic's "Pump Up the Jam" or "Move This" would work too, I concede.] The piece — sound and slides — lasts as long as the song does.)*

(Text, on Slides)

The performer is supposed to be a go-go boy, like those found in those deep, dark, sleazy bars of Thailand.

But you wouldn't know anything about that, would you now?

In actuality, a real go-go boy wouldn't have all those tattoos.

So, if you could, please imagine the performer without all those tattoos.

Also, a proper go-go boy wouldn't be quite so flabby.

So, if you could, please imagine the performer a little trimmer and a little slimmer, please.

(The Voice-Over)

Another day of shaking my ass in front of these nonchalantly horny tourists.

Hmm, wonder if any of the regulars are going to show up today?

God, I hope I get good tips today.

Pump up the jam, pump it up, pump pump it jam, ride on time ride on time...

Attack of the Man-Eating Lotus Blossoms

And a true go-go boy would have fluffier hair. You know what to do.

And while you're at it, please use your imagination to make the performer's skin much silkier.

Silkier please.

More silky dammit! What the fuck's wrong with your imagination?

Okay. That's silky enough. You can stop now.

The performer bought this thong in 1989 from the International Male catalog.

He was in his office at the university filling out the order form when he was visited by Mari Matsuoka, the angry communist from hell, who wanted to complain about something the Imperial Capitalist Patriarchal White Male Bush adminstration was doing to indigenous people of color.

At that time in his life, he liked to lie in the sun. The thong was his attempt to reduce tan-lines.

"To Do" List

1. Call Mom.

2. Wash towels behind bathroom door.

3. Buy cat food, Friskies not Meow Mix. Remember to get Pilchards in Aspic 'cos she likes that.

4. ...let's see... Oh yes, get passport photos.

5. Return video tapes to Billy.

6. Return library books. Shit, I have $6.50 in fines now...

Hmm, what should I have for dinner...?

I believe Cher, I believe!

A month later, International Male released the Tan-Thru Bikini Swimsuit™. He was happy.

He has since given that activity up.

Right now, the thong is giving him the worst case of Portuguese Butt Torture.

Hey, isn't that new Cher album really great?

While not completely naked, this is the first time in his career that the performer has taken off this much clothing onstage. He is feeling really self-conscious right now.

Please do not look.

He should have elected to do the naked performance artist thing earlier in the '90s. When he was younger. And when all that body performance art stuff was in vogue.

If you read that last slide, you were looking when you were specifically instructed not to look.

The performer will pretend that you are like doctors so that he will feel comfortable.

In efforts to describe universal human behavior by cataloging cultural differences, practitioners of anthropology have done a great deal to fill out the category of the traditional.

...however, when ethnography actually confronts the modern at home, it all too frequently fails to recognize it as other than that which has imagined home far afield that.... Ooo, have to remember the recipe for chili crabs that Lori gave me.

Okay, 2 katis of crabs, cleaned and cut, 2 eggs,

some oil, ginger, garlic, red chilis, sugar, salt

and ketchup, of course...

Heat the oil until very hot and then stir-fry the crabs for two minutes...

Remember to crack the claws beforehand so that flavor can seep in...

Attack of the Man-Eating Lotus Blossoms

The performer is sucking in his stomach by the way.

Take a picture, it'll last longer. No wait, don't take any pictures.

In this thong and in this vulnerable state, I can feel someone in the audience's childhood pain.

Something to do with being age seven, some disconnect with the father figure. Am I right?

All this undulating is really really painful.

This is the last slide for this section.

On medium heat, fry the ginger, garlic, and chilis. Then quickly add to the crab. Add the sugar, salt and ketchup. Bring to a boil, lower fire...

Wait a minute, what do I do with the eggs? Have to call her again.

I wonder what's going through these peoples' minds, right now?

I, Documentary,
or, I Buy a Camera and Document My Love Life

(The performer is seated with a box of photographs on his lap. Where indicated in the text, he holds up a photograph and looks nostalgically at it.

Or better yet:
The performer is seated on the floor. A deluge of photographs comes showering down, some fluttering, some dead-dropping on him from somewhere above. He looks a bit bewildered and on his hands and knees starts to sift and poke among the photographs, mumbling [audibly] "I'm looking for a photograph, have you seen it around here?" He finds the photograph; his demeanor changes instantly.)

This is Jeff. We met when I was still very young and naïve. This is a picture of Jeff and me when we were vacationing in the desert.

This is a picture of Jeff with a bad sunburn. Jeff was really sweet and fun-loving and we had a good eight months together before he went mad. They said it was chemical, something hereditary.

This is a picture of Jeff being admitted to the psych ward. It was very sad. But at the hospital, I met Wayne. He was the orderly. I knew instantly he was capable of caring.

This is a picture of Wayne. He was really cute and so giving. This is a picture of him moving in. No wait, it's a picture of him moving out. Yeah, it just wasn't working out after a while, and maybe we rushed it a little.

But this is Ernie. He was one of the movers who helped Wayne move out. We dated for a while. But then he was still in love with his ex. So of course, it didn't work out.

So after all that, I decided to go into group therapy. This is a picture of the whole group. And there I met Steve. He was more fucked up than I was and so, naturally, we found each other. At first I thought his neuroses were kind of cute and kind of challenging, but then it started to get annoying faster than I thought. I stopped going to group therapy when we broke up.

That's when I met Kelly at the dentist's office. This is a picture of him at his desk. We dated for a while. He liked men with mustaches and I just could not grow one.

We decided to mutually call it quits. On the bus home, I met Rufus. He was really quite sweet, but a little needy. A lot needy. A full-on-slut needy.

We decided on an open relationship. One day, we went to the sex club together and I met Ishmael. I guess my relationship with Ishmael was more of a sexual thing. Now I know that but then, we were madly in love, but the language difficulties got

Attack of the Man-Eating Lotus Blossoms

in the way. He spoke mostly Croatian and very little English, and it was a miracle we even lasted for those seven months.

Then at the Serbo-Croat Translation Center trying to explain to Ishmael about the breakup, I met Danny. This is a picture of him and his bird. He had a parrot, and I hated parrots, and he was allergic to cats, so that did not work out.

But then I started up with Rufus again after we bumped into each other at the Chaka Khan concert. How we laughed about that. This is a picture of us at the concert; oh, we look so happy. This time, we decided to have a closed relationship.

That was a mistake because we were always jealous, all the time. This is a picture of Rufus and me at Rick and Robin's house for Christmas dinner. Look how happy we all are, smiling and acting silly.

Robin was a massage therapist and we started screwing around for a couple of months. Which made Rufus and Rick really mad and then Robin got all upset and said that he couldn't massage me anymore.

Now I had to go to the community health massage clinic. And there I met Jack. By this time Rufus had moved back to Idaho. Here's a picture of him driving off in the U-Haul with Rick.

Jack was nice, but he was married. To a woman. We had an affair for a few months and then he decided to be straight again. It was fun though. This is a picture of Jack, his wife, Shirley, her officemate Steve, and me at a picnic in Golden Gate Park. She was a really nice woman.

This is a picture of Steve in bed. We had a good time with each other, but then he left to go to New York to do his play and I never heard from him again. Or of any of his plays.

These are pictures of the wicker baskets that Jeff made when he was home recuperating from his breakdown. Jeff made very good wicker baskets. He learned weaving as a mental health exercise. The baskets were selling very well at Pier One, which bought them on consignment. The psych ward said he was no danger to himself or anyone. I'm glad.

After Jeff was discharged, we started spending a lot of time together. But then he decided to go to a racialist vegan commune in Oregon. This is a picture of the goodbye wicker basket he made for me.

But I'm okay about it, as long as he's happy and taking care of himself. One day at Pier One, looking at Jeff's baskets, I met Jonathon. He was thirty-five but still lived with his parents. At that time, I mistook that for some level of stability that I was missing in my life. Boy, was I wrong. This is a picture of Jonathon crying when I said I couldn't see him anymore. His mom knocked on his door to ask if everything was okay. She left sandwiches and cookies at the door for us. She was nice.

After Jonathon, I wanted to take some time off from dating, but then I met Barry at the photo-developing kiosk. I don't know, it's only been a few weeks, but I think it's going to work out, I think this might be the one...

The Sarong Party Gay Boy

(In the manner of a university lecture, or voice-of-God–style documentary film.)

> **NARRATOR:** Who is the Sarong Party Gay Boy?
> Contrary to his name, the Sarong Party Gay Boy does not wear a sarong. The sarong is only used as a defense mechanism to blend into his surroundings when there is a threat from another Sarong Party Gay Boy.
> First spotted in the famed Orchard Road district in Singapore in the '80s, hanging out at the Hilton Hotel, at TGI Fridays, and at Brannigans, he has since spread out to all parts of the globe. Today, he can be found all over the world. Sociologists are still baffled by his migratory patterns.

Attack of the Man-Eating Lotus Blossoms

Let's find out more from a noted French Expert:

SLIDE:

> **NOTED FRENCH EXPERT**
> **(notice the Goatee of Authority)**

(The performer puts on a fake goatee and a beret and holds a baguette.)

FRENCH EXPERT: *(He speaks with a heavy French accent.)* Zee Szarong Parteegae Boi ees by hees na'chture migratoree. Hee achieevez deez by looring ay hozt andz by allsorts of williez and voo doo mating dancez vif hees szarong, heeswill attache heeself tozee hozt, and eef zee circumstazes tzurn out right, zee hozt vill aid zee Szarong Parteegae Boi een hees na'chtureal migratoree eenstinctz. Een heez nu groundz, zee Szarong Parteegae Boi vill shed heez szarong and proceed to partee. If heeneedz to moove to anothzer plaze, hee vil don szee szarong a-gain to loure a hozt. Hozt of zee Szarong Parteegae Boi are uzually Kenz, Hanzes, and Bobz.

ENGLISH TRANSLATION: "The Sarong Party Gay Boy is by his nature migratory. He achieves this by luring a host and by all sorts of willies and voodoo-mating dances with his sarong, he will attach himself to the host, and if the circumstances turn out right, the host will aid the Sarong Party Gay Boy in his natural migratory instincts. In his new ground, the Sarong Party Gay boy will shed his sarong and proceed to party. If he needs to move to another place, he will don the sarong again to lure a host. Hosts of the Sarong Party Gay Boy are usually Kens, Hans, and Bobs."

TRANSLATED TO KOREAN, THEN RETRANSLATED TO ENGLISH USING AN ONLINE SERVICE: "Per the Sarong Boy who is cheerful is the rambling side his character. He tempts the host various willies and a friendship magic and attains this. So he mates and gives in his company old bravery he does, he attaches in the host. His natural enemy situation passes and when it is puts out, the host will assist Per the Sarong Boy rambling instinct who will be cheerful inside. Inside his new ground, Per the Sarong boy in the sugar who is cheerful to spill his company. It moves toward the place where he is different, the fact that in necessity in order to tempt the host he is to extend company to old Mister again. The host of Per the Sarong Boy is cheerful and the Kens and the Hans and it is a Bob."

TRANSLATED TO CHINESE, THEN RETRANSLATED TO ENGLISH USING AN ONLINE SERVICE: "The Sarong Amusement Joyful Boy is migrates by his essence. He achieved this by lure the host computer and teaches by various willies to join dances with his sarong, he will attach the oneself on host computer, and if the situation result, the host will help the Sarong Amusement Joyful Boy in his nature migration instinct. In his new ground, the Sarong Amusement Joyful Boy will shed his sarong and carries on to the amusement. If he needs to move out to other arrangements, he will don sarong to lure the host again. The Sarong Amusement Joyful Boy's host usually is willing Hans and suddenly moves."

TRANSLATED TO DUTCH, THEN RETRANSLATED TO FRENCH, THEN RETRANSLATED TO GREEK, AND THEN RETRANSLATED TO ENGLISH, USING AN ONLINE SERVICE: "The cheerful boy of contracting part sarong is migratoring from his nature. Reaches in this trying also entertained from all types of groin of will and contact dances with sarong. This entertained connects also as just progress of circumstance. The entertained cheerful boy of contracting part sarong will help sarong in his natural migrants instincts. In his new impurity, the cheerful boy of contracting part sarong throw you also in the contracting part, that goes to work. If it should move in other placement, it will attract again sarong to try entertained. Entertained the

Attack of the Man-Eating Lotus Blossoms

cheerful boy of contracting part sarong are know usually by Hans and load jest."

TRANSLATE TO YOUR NATIVE LANGUAGE OR YOUR FAVORITE LANGUAGE HERE: _____
_____
_____
_____
_____
_____
_____
_____
_____

TRANSLATE TO CUNEIFORM OR CAVE PAINTINGS HERE:

NARRATOR: Here, the Sarong Party Gay Boy is re-enacting a scene from his favorite movie, *Indecent Proposal*. He too dreams that one day someone will make an indecent proposal to him. His answer will be *Okay!*

(The performer lolls on the floor tossing and rubbing money all over himself as if sponge-bathing.)

The Sarong Party Gay Boy dreams of going to:
— The United States
(The performer holds up a mini U.S. flag and a McDonald's Apple Pie.)
— The U.K.
(The performer holds up a mini U.K. flag and a cuppa tea.)

—France
(The performer holds up a mini French flag and a bag of l'oignon and a hulk of le fromage.)
—Germany
(The performer holds up a mini German flag and a knockwurst or something suitably Germanic.)
—and Australia
(The performer holds up a mini Aussie flag and a kangaroo. Or a can of Foster's, or a boomerang.)

If the Sarong Party Gay Boy knows anything, it is the European (i.e., Western) penis.

Today, we have a Sarong Party Gay Boy who, using a Samsung Compact Series MW2000U microwave oven, and a pack of Ball Park Franks, will take us on a fascinating tour of the distinctive characteristics of the Western penis.

(The performer whips off a black drape on the table revealing a microwave. A pack of Ball Park Franks hot dogs sits beside it. The performer chucks the package, with its plastic wrapper still on, into the microwave and turns the dial. The sausages cook for two minutes, finishing in a bright alarm bell. Using chopsticks, he proceeds to eat the franks in accompaniment to the narrator's descriptions. One frank for each description, and each frank is eaten in its entirety.)

SLIDE:

> **The German Penis**
> **(Das Schlong)**

NARRATOR: The German Penis. Please notice the bulging head, the heft, and how pale it looks, how guilt-ridden, don't bring up the war with this schlong.

SLIDE:

> **The French Penis**
> **(Le Wee-Wee)**

Attack of the Man-Eating Lotus Blossoms

NARRATOR: The French Penis. Please notice the smooth shaft, it is sometimes a little saucy and slightly pungent, and always so nationalistic.

SLIDE:

> **The British Penis**
> **(The Imperial Poker, or, The Queen Mum)**

NARRATOR: The British Penis. Please notice how it curves slightly, that is the postcolonial droop. It is tangy with a hint of Stilton, and it cannot be trusted to behave at football matches.

SLIDE:

> **The Italian Penis**
> **(Il Salami)**

NARRATOR: The Italian Penis. Please notice the very distinct shape, its rowdy nature, its amorous cling. It is well garlicky, of course.

SLIDE:

> **The Spanish Penis**
> **(El Pee-pee)**

NARRATOR: The Spanish Penis. Please notice how forceful it looks, it is always looking for a bull to fight or a siesta in your bed. But you can wake it up. See how it insists on being noticed.

SLIDE:

> **The Scandinavian Penis**
> **(Torval)**

NARRATOR: The Scandinavian Penis. Please notice how it retracts on itself. Myth has it that its helmet has horns, but you can see that it doesn't. See how frosty it is, how cool it is on the outside, but so warm and oozy on the inside.

SLIDE:

> **The Aussie Penis**
> **(The 'Roo)**

NARRATOR: The Aussie Penis. Please notice how it hangs, how bouncy it is. How it is loud and obnoxious and loves to sing bawdy pub songs. It loves nothing more than to soak in malted barley. There is a hint of eucalyptus to this one.

SLIDE:

> **The American Penis (Bruce, or, The Threat of Military Invasion and Subsequent Colonization to Spread the Tenets of Capitalism Disguised as Democracy)**

NARRATOR: The American Penis. Please notice how militaristic it looks, almost as if it wants to dominate you. Also notice the distinctive head, this one follows very well, unquestioningly. Its flavor is way too sweet, of course, but it is also available in diet, decaffeinated, lo-carb, cherry, lemon; and you can charge it to your VISA/AMEX.

Wasn't that fascinating. Like Darwin's finches, the Sarong Party Gay Boy has adapted himself to the penises in his surroundings. We hope that this presentation has familiarized you somewhat with the Sarong Party Gay Boy. Now if you see him on your streets, do show him your penis for scientific purposes. We'll see you again next week, when we explore what the Sarong Party Gay Boy knows about European asses.

Attack of the Man-Eating Lotus Blossoms

So Solo

(This piece can be performed using any play or film script. I usually oscillate between Kubrick's Eyes Wide Shut *and Hitchcock's* Vertigo. *Essentially, a character from a movie or play is selected and then the performer proceeds to perform or read all the lines for that character as if it were a monologue. In* Eyes Wide Shut, *it's Nicole Kidman's character Alice; and in* Vertigo, *how can one not choose Kim Novak's character Madeleine/Judy? The lines are read with a bit of a tempo, a bit of a beat, slightly faster than regular speech but doesn't go into the realms of a dramatic performance just yet. Tonally, I tend to favor a deadpan monotonous voice, or sometimes a rushed warbly reading interrupted only by running out of air in the lungs and having to gasp and gulp down more.)*

Butterfly

(The performer is dressed in a kimono. Or a slutty cheongsam, but that is redundant, all cheongsams are made to look slutty. The tape starts: it is a mixed tape of the famed aria from Puccini's Madame Butterfly, *but digitally fucked up so it warbles, speeds up, and occasionally segues into the Bee Gee's "Tragedy," though The Steps cover is much more suitable for the purpose of this performance.*

The performer is slumped on the floor. He dramatically crawls and claws his way across stage to an utterly unbelievably oriental headdress and puts it on. The headdress seems to stir something in him, but not quite enough. Once again, he dramatically half-drags half-crawls himself across the stage, this time reaching for a small container. It is a powder puff. With great flourishes, he uses the puff and powders his face flour-white, and using a fingertip moistened with diet cola [any flavor, any brand], he touches his lips ever so lightly. Think of it as ghetto geisha lip-lining. Think of it as Wal-Mart Geisha Unextreme Makeover.

Thus rejuvenated, with great aplomb, he hurls his tragic body to the table fan sitting at one side of the stage and turns it on, letting his kimono billow melodramatically for a few moments. The performer then flings his poor pitiful body across the stage and picks up a whisk, realizes what it is, and flings it away in disgust. He picks up another utensil, but it is a cocktail fork, and he flings it away with more disgust. He picks up a small knife, looks satisfied for a moment, then flings that away in contempt, and picks up a bigger knife. He looks at the knife forlornly.

With the knife in hand, the performer then flings his even more pitiful and more tragic body across the stage where he picks up a whole red watermelon that is wrapped in a shawl. Is it a pashmina? We wonder. We stop wondering when he dramatically flings the shawl aside and picks up the melon as if it were his child and weeps. Throwing the knife away, he rushes to look for an even bigger, more dramatic, more dangerous knife. He finds it. The performer returns center stage, and with the watermelon cradled against his belly as if he were pregnant, he plunges the knife into the melon, committing seppuku, or is it abortion? [Who knows? The drama and tragedy is too great for details like that now.] The cut is made in a gouging manner, so the red insides of the watermelon are exposed to the audience. As the tape crescendos and climaxes, the performer keels over and dies. All the while, the headdress remains firmly in place.)

COCKFIGHT

justin chin & hung nguyen

In new stunning collaboration performance, COCKFIGHT is a duel of words, images and the subconscious.

From sex clubs to playgrounds, from karaoke bars to refugee camps, COCKFIGHT takes you on a whirlwind journey through the American ideals of homeland and freedom, showing that the reality behind the cultural souvenirs are deeper, more personal and more universal than a package holiday in the tropics will ever allow.

**Highways Performance Space: 1651 18th St. Santa Monica
JUNE 7-8 (Sat.-Sun.) & 12-13 (Thu.-Fri), 8:30 pm**
Tickets $12. For reservations, call Tickets LA : 213-660-8587

Little Demons
(Odd Bits and Unrealized Performance Pieces)

Slab (1995-1997)

I was performing *Slab* in the storefront window at Artists' Television Access, which looks out onto Valencia Street in San Francisco's Mission District. A very harried woman with her child in tow rushed up to the door of ATA, and pounded on it until a staffer answered the door. She pushed her way in and said, "I have to explain what's going on in that window to my child." The staffer calmly explained performance art to her, briefly stating its governing ideas and goals. "Oh, okay, okay," she said impatiently. Then turning to her child, I heard her say, "Ruben, this is what is known as kinky art. It's what people do when they want attention." And then, with a huff, she galloped out the doors, dragging Ruben down the street with her.

***

(The performer is strapped into a straitjacket and his legs are tied together at the ankles. A hood, preferably one of those leather S/M masks where all you can see are the eyes and mouth, is placed over the performer's head. Everything is strapped down tight.

The performer is tossed or dragged into the performance space. Elaborately wrapped gift boxes are either placed in the space or brought to the performer, who attempts to open his presents with whatever means are available to him. Usually, this involves gnawing on the wrapper and ripping it, or bashing it in with his head and body against the floor, or a combination of both. Inside each of the gift boxes is a lump of cooked rice. When the performer succeeds in opening the box and revealing the rice lump, he then proceeds to eat it off the floor.

The piece ends either (1) at a designated time, when someone comes and drags the performer away by his ankles; or (2) when there are no more boxes left to open, and no more rice left to eat.)

Justin Chin

From Cockfight (1998)

In 1998, I collaborated with performance artist Hung Nguyen, who was then based in Los Angeles. It wasn't the most relaxing process, especially for any artist who till then had worked solo (and was full of Virgo-tainted obsessive compulsiveness), but it was a process I enjoyed tremendously, especially given how different we were. While Hung was comfortable running around stark naked and being all spiritual and self-actualized, I was putting on a hooded parka and gloves, and roiling in my ever-profane funk, filled with doubt and self-pity.

What I loved about the shows we did was how we used the performance space visually and how it was turned into something that constantly sparked little moments of beauty and wonder:

• A row of rice cookers actively cooking rice while the performance was in progress, filling the space with its lovely fragrance, that familiar smell of home.

• Scores of long kite tails hanging from the rafters which billowed when the table fan on the floor was switched on. Hung made a kite and flew it indoors. And later, during the performance, we lit a number of those kite tails and watched the fire spiral its way up as onion-skin-thin layers of ash floated down. (Highways in Santa Monica was such an amazing place, so open and committed to the artist's vision, that they allowed you to do almost anything provided that you cleaned up afterward and did not raze the building to the ground.) Otherwise, the plan was to keep the fire thing hush-hush until the show itself. We did take a lot of precautions: making specific tails to burn which had a fire-break in them, flame-retarding everything around, making sure the tails were clear of lights.

• A scrim made from dressmaker patterns.

• In one of Hung's solo pieces, a piece remembering his childhood years in the refugee camp, he slicked the stage with

Attack of the Man-Eating Lotus Blossoms

water and threw himself across the stage, playfully sliding back and forth. Then later, we had concocted a small contraption that, when triggered on cue, would send a trickle of sand falling from the ceiling.

A lot of the show was unscripted as such, and we improvised our speeches and dialogue based on certain talking points and guidelines that we had plotted and agreed on prior. Again, this is not how I normally work, given how much I put my trust in the text; more than a few anxiety attacks were had. But that's the great thing about collaborating: you get cajoled to do things you normally wouldn't choose to; you get to thinking in different ways.

To calm those anxious moments then, I had to write something down, and the three pieces collected here are part of that.

***

1. Who The Rice!
(The two performers sit on chairs down stage. There is a rice cooker in between them. It is an actual working cooker and rice has been cooking in it until this moment. J serves up the rice in bowls. There is a small stash of eating utensils, all kinds and manner of spoons, sporks, forks, and chopsticks, behind the back of the chair, and the performers very nonchalantly, very casually switch off on eating utensils — individually and with each other during the piece.)

    J: *(in Chinese)* Time to eat!
    H: *(in Vietnamese)* Time to eat!
    J: How's your rice?
    H: Good. And how's yours.
    J: Good. *(pause)* So, Hung, I want to ask you something. Sometimes when you're lying in bed late at night, do you sometimes wonder what kind of rice you would be, if you were rice?
    H: No. I never think that. Do you?
    J: No. *(pause)* Okay, well sometimes, I think I might be Jasmine. Or maybe Basmati.
    H: I know what you mean. Sometimes I think I might

be Brown Rice.

J: Oh my god, that's so fibrous. Once I was thinking about what kind of rice I would be and I fell asleep and I had a nightmare. I dreamt I was Rice-A-Roni. It was horrible: I woke up and my heart was palpitating like mad and I was crying.

H: How horrible. But you could have been Uncle Ben's Boil-in-the-Bag, which is worse, so flavorless, bad texture *(both shudder)*. This rice is really good.

J: Yes, not too sticky, not too dry. *(They eat.)* Hung, I have something else I need to ask you. Okay, when you're lying in bed at night imagining that you're rice, do you like... I'm not sure how to put this...do you ever imagine what sort of side dishes and entrees would be served with you?

H: NO! That's weird, man! Do you think of such thing?

J: Oh no no! That is really weird. *(Pause.)* Okay, sometimes I think there will be a good pork dish. I think that suckling pig would be good, but then you don't really eat that with rice, so that's kind of queer. But maybe some eng-chai with sambal belachan, and maybe chili crabs, or a good curry.

H: I think I would have *(ad-libs a list of Vietnamese dishes)*.

J: Ooo, good choice. *(They eat some more.)* So, Hung...do you wonder who will do the dishes later?

2. *The Rice Bowl*

(The performers stand behind their chairs.)

(voice-over): Welcome to the final rounds of Rice Bowl XXXXVII. Our two remaining finalists are Hung Nguyen, representing Vietnam and Los Angeles; and Justin Chin, representing Malaysia and San Francisco. The two contestants have battled their way to this point, and this is the moment of truth. Soon, you, the audience, by your applause, will have the tough job of deciding the winner of Rice Bowl XXXXVII.

Are the contestants ready? You have three minutes. GO!

(Both performers rush to the row of rice cookers and dig out huge clumps of rice with their bare hands. They bring the rice back to the

Attack of the Man-Eating Lotus Blossoms

chair and on the seat of the chair start working the rice, sculpting it into a sculpture [of sorts].

A timer goes off. Each performer takes turns introducing his piece and what it means. Dedications and shout-outs included.)

(*voice-over*): Now, audience, it's time for you to decide the winner of Rice Bowl XXXXVII. By your applause... Will it be *(spotlight falls on one performer)* [applause]? Or will it be *(spotlight on other performer)* [applause]? *(Dramatic pause.)* YOU THE AUDIENCE HAVE DECIDED! The winner of Rice Bowl XXXXVII is.... *(Spotlight falls on the performer who has garnered more applause.*

The winner takes a bow. While cheesy music plays, the loser slumps over to the winner's sculpture and proceeds to eat it.)

3. XXXSEXACT

SLIDE:

> **Write Your Name on My Ass with a Marker Pen. $2**

(The performer solicits a member from the audience who wants to or agrees to the advertised act. That audience member is dragged onstage, seated, and handed a Sharpie. The performer tells him to practice his signature or handwriting, since there's only one shot at this. The performer announces that he's going to get his ass ready. He runs offstage and returns with a stuffed donkey. The donkey is already covered in handwriting. The audience member adds his name to any part of the donkey.)

"My Ass."

Justin Chin

Demon Share (a speculative performance)

Flipping through my notebooks, I remembered that I was thinking about possibly doing a performance work titled *Demon Share*. *Demon Share* would be about demon possession and exorcism and using that as a trope to explore illness and mortality, specifically the HIV virus as something that possesses a body like a demon would.

※※※

*Notes for **Demon Share**:*

"I cannot believe this demon in you. I cannot believe that every drop of your blood, every tear, each time you kiss me, each time you sweat and cry and laugh, each taste I take of you is filled with this devil, this Lucifer, this demon that will not begone."

(1. Using hooks, or bungee cords, two hooks grip into the sides of the performer's mouth. The retractable cords pull a little, a slight tension so that the mouth is seemingly being pulled apart, poking into the cheek. First image seen when lights up. The performer answers [or attempts to answer] questions while this contraption is in place.

2. While performing monologue, wear very very tight pants and proceed to do deep knee bends until the pants start to rip apart.

3. Sit in front of a VERY harsh light and be interviewed, or answer questions. Expect to squint, sweat, and be temporarily blinded when segment is over and houselights are down. Work the spots seen in this state into a small monologue that follows.

4. Questions/Interview are about life and death, illness and disease, pain and tolerance of it, fear, mortality, the afterlife, with a few curveballs and a few oddballs thrown in.

> *Examples:*
> *What are you scared of?*
> *How do you think you will die?*

Attack of the Man-Eating Lotus Blossoms

What do you think is the most painful way to die?
Chicken or beef?
Would you rather lose an arm or a leg?
Would you rather be shot or stabbed?
Have you ever been attacked by a wild animal?
What is the sickest you've ever been?
What is your most irrational fear?
Are you scared of sock puppets?

5. On sock-puppet question, sock puppets slowly descend from the ceiling and hang just beside or behind the performer at eye level. After answering the questions, he puts his hands into the sock puppet.

6. Slide: The performer responds to criticism that he is not incorporating enough of his culture and ethnic heritage into his performance work.
    Announces that he will do Wayang Kulit, the traditional Balinese/Indonesian shadow-puppet play.
    Goes behind screen [rigged with rear light] and uses sock puppets as the puppets in the play. Then the light source changes and it is the Martina Navratilova Work-Out Tape or Barbie Work-Out Tape, or rather its projection that is the light source. The plays turns out to be Jarry's Ubu roi.

7. Possible lighting source/object. Place a working flashlight in an airtight Ziploc bag and seal it properly. Drop bag with flashlight into a larger glass jar filled with water [experiment with other fluids as well]. Try piling a mound of salt over the whole thing, see if effect changes.)

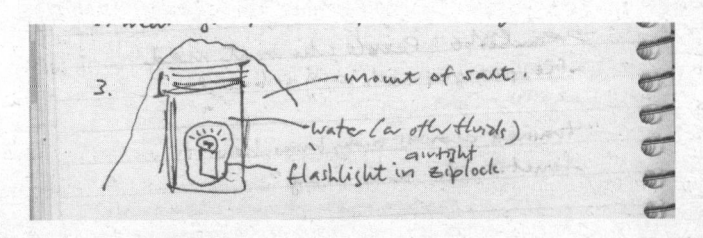

(letters)

Bad Asian

I am not a political person, but the other day something happened that made me so angry that I must get it off my chest.

I saw an advertisement in the newspaper for a play called *And Judas Boogied Until His Slippers Wept*, by someone named Justin Chin. I thought, "Great, finally there is a play by a gay Asian man!"

But what a shock I had when I went to the play! It was awful. He constantly referred to himself as a fag, a queer and as a Chink. He also talked about suicide, molestation, non-loving sex and other negative things. But worst of all, in a section called "9-7-CHINK" he made gay Asians look really bad. As if gay Asians do not face enough prejudice and hatred in this world! Many gay Asians have worked hard to fit into gay society and have been accepted by mainstream society. For Justin Chin to make such ugly and negative images is an insult to all gay Asians.

I am a proud gay Asian American. I am not a Chink. I am not a fag. Justin Chin is a bad person. I left his show feeling like I wanted to vomit. I was so sad and angry and disappointed. I hope the people at Josie's will pick a better, more positive play, like ▇▇▇ show last year; it was so much more positive that I could even bring my parents to it. That represents the real gay Asian-American community that should be shown next time.

San Francisco